Joe + Lori

Enjoy

Swine on the Reach

Swine on the Reach

A Novel

Frank Ombres

VANTAGE PRESS
New York

This is a work of fiction. Any similarity between the names and characters in this book and any real persons, living or dead, is purely coincidental.

FIRST EDITION

All rights reserved, including the right of reproduction in whole or in part in any form.

Copyright © 2007 by Frank Ombres

Published by Vantage Press, Inc.
419 Park Ave. South, New York, NY 10016

Manufactured in the United States of America
ISBN: 0-533-15752-5

Library of Congress Catalog Card No.: 2007901522

0 9 8 7 6 5 4 3 2 1

Teresa. Allie.

Swine on the Reach

One
Aahk, Aahk, Aahk, Aahk

"Seth lost his *dick*?" she asked incredulously.

"That's what they're saying," her best friend answered.

"What about . . . ?"

"Those too!"

"And they can't be reattached?"

"Can't find em," she said, barely able to hide her smile any more.

"Will he live?"

"Yeah, he'll live. I hope he lives for a long time." Smiling broadly now at the thought of Seth Meshitsky and the miserable life that lay ahead of him. Thinking back two years to the incident in Bunny's outdoor shower, an involuntary shudder overcame her. To this day, still humiliated.

"Too bad about his father, though," her friend said, lying.

"Yeah, too bad." Joining in the lie.

"Incredible. The whole thing is just infuckingcredible!" Their attention now on two seagulls maybe fifteen yards away, near the surf. The tide going out. The last tide of the unofficial end of the summer season on this Labor Day afternoon, 1994. The gulls were fighting over what looked to be a half-eaten sandwich still partially wrapped in foil. The smaller of the two, speckled grey in its coloring, was clearly outmaneuvering its much larger, handsomer, pure white rival. It skitted this way and that, deftly jumping back and forth, protecting the goods. The large gull seemed ready to give up the contest when the grey one rose a few feet carrying the food with it. As if the large white gull knew what was about to happen, it stayed on the beach gazing upward as the sandwich separated from the torn wrapping and dropped directly into its waiting, gaping beak. The large graceful bird then spread its wings and took off with its prize, disappearing beyond the dunes. The grey gull, having lost the battle returned down to the ground, poked at the foil in vain for any scraps and, finding none, began a series of shrieking cackles. An announcement of defeat. *AAHK, AAHK, AAHK, AAHK.*

The girls watched the drama play out and when the gull started cackling they looked at each other, knowing they were thinking the same thing. One of them laughed. A small laugh. Unintentional but unstoppable. Now laughing from the other girl. Putting her hands over her mouth, feigning an attempt to stop. The laughter growing loud and uncontrollable now from both of them. Eyes tearing, holding their stomachs, rolling on the blanket unable to stop. When they finally gained control it didn't last. Just one look at each other and they erupted again and didn't stop until one of them, followed closely by the other, scampered and stumbled, still laughing so hard it almost hurt, their arms outstretched trying to clasp hands as they plunged into the surf just as the pee began trickling down their thighs. Only after regaining their composure and making their way back to their spot on the sand did they notice the little old lady with a big straw sunhat. She was watching them from a bench at one of the many breaks in the jagged dune line that led from the beach to the streets of Reach Island, southern New Jersey's answer to the Riviera, and the closest thing to paradise the northeast had to offer. The lady waved to them with a gesture that told them she knew what prompted their laughing fit and that it was okay. Embarrassed anyway, the girls returned the wave.

J'net

Pretty girls, those two. Nineteen, maybe twenty I'd say. Hightailin' it into the water as fast as they could, probably tryin' to make it in before they wet their bikini bottoms, what little of em there was to wet in the first place. Lord, the suits can't get any smaller. Nothin' left to the imagination, as the sayin' goes. I swear, three or four band aids in the right spots might cover more. Times sure have changed since I was their age. Course, I shouldn't be surprised, it is almost sixty years! Can't blame em for laughin' like that, though. Had a hard time keepin' it in myself. I suppose you'd be hard-pressed to find anybody who ain't heard what happened yesterday by now. And not too many I'll bet who ain't giddy with delight. Well, I suppose that might be an exaggeration. But not much of one. My, what a day it was. And what a night! I don't know when the Reach saw anything like it before. Probably never. Amazin' how peaceful and quiet it is today after all that commotion. Police. Probably the whole force judgin' by the number of em. Ambulances. Fire trucks too, though of course there wasn't no fire. Even above all the noise of those sirens you could still hear the little bastard cacklin' like a seagull. Only this time he wasn't laughin' about it like the pain in the ass he usually is. No, this time it was different. At first you couldn't tell cause he was too far out on the bay, I guess. Everybody naturally assumed he was just bein' his normal annoyin' little-bastard self. There was no ignorin' it either. Everything happenin' like it did right in the middle of the big block party and all. I sure hope what transpired last night doesn't mean the end of the annual block parties. That would be a shame. Actually, if you think about it, they'd be much improved now if you want to know the plain truth. No, the *block parties shouldn't end. Lord, the food just keeps gettin' better and better every year. So does the wine. Joe surely loved tastin' all the block party wines. He so looked forward to it every year, rest his soul. Anyway, it was loud, though. The cacklin' I mean. And real painful soundin'. And he wouldn't stop. Couldn't, I suppose. That's when someone realized it wasn't his laughin' cackle at all, but sort of a wailin' kind of cackle like maybe he was in excruciatin' pain. And that he was. Anyway, he didn't stop his new-soundin' cackle till he was passed out in the ambulance half way off the Island on the way to the hospital. He might still not even know if his father's dead or alive. Or care for that matter. Except for the money. Course, that's a whole other story, ain't it? Yes, it surely is. Looks like the girls are gettin' ready to leave. Summer's over. Time to pack away the tiny bikinis till next year and head back to school. Wherever that is. Bye kids, have a good winter! Nice smiles. Nice lookin' kids, both of em. Surprised they even know the little bastard. Course, the little bastard ain't so little no more. Maybe they just know <u>of</u> him. That's probably it. Well, summer's over for me too. Half the season's bulgin' population is most likely leavin' today. The rest'll be gone in the next few days, me with em. Only difference is I wont be comin' back. No, I've put three husbands in the ground, the best not six months ago. I shouldn't say that. I shouldn't even think it. They was all three of em the best there ever was. It's just Joe was the last, so it makes him sorta special right now. And here on the Reach is where he passed and I don't think I want to be reminded of that every day. No, I'm goin' back to where we met twelve years ago. Another little piece of paradise in another part of the world. My stepson lives there, so it'll be good. Joe would be happy with that. But I'll miss the people here. Especially most of those at Bay Vista. That's "Most" with a capital M. Maybe I'll come back every year for the block party. If they continue. And if I'm up to it. We'll see. But I'm really gonna miss this Island. I'm gonna miss the Reach.*

Two
The Reach

Reach Island is a barrier island that stretches for sixteen miles along the Atlantic coastline, sitting about four miles off the New Jersey mainland. At its midpoint is a two-lane causeway, the Island's only access or egress other than by boat. From that midpoint on it hooks slightly east, widening the distance from the mainland to about five miles at the southern end. The name was derived from its earliest visitors and settlers who, in the beginning of the nineteenth century, would venture across the bay to its southernmost tip in all manner of craft, many of which were no match for the unpredictable currents and sudden shoals that made that inlet one of the most dangerous on the eastern seaboard. So treacherous was it that just to "*reach*" the Island safely in those days was no small feat. People would set out to *reach the Island* originally just for hunting and fishing adventure. It wasn't too long before settlers arrived, and commerce began to develop soon thereafter. This paved the way for vacationers, primarily wealthy Philadelphians seeking the cool ocean breezes that the shore offered during hot summer months. They'd escape the oppressive city to *reach the Island*.

Over time, *reach the Island,* as in something one would do, became *Reach Island,* as in somewhere one would go. Those earliest settlements at the southern end slowly and steadily expanded northward to the rest of the Island. Today the Island is home to a small, yet ever-growing few and a bustling, vibrant resort destination for many, many more. And today it's known simply as the *Reach*. The Island's population increased twenty fold in the summer months with an influx of people that fell into three general categories. The largest of these groups were called the *transients*—families, some vacationing here for the first time and others who returned year after year to rent homes all over the Island, for a week or two or more, some for the entire season. The second group was known as the *summer residents*—those with enough money to be able to own a second home at the shore.

Then, like in beach towns everywhere, there were the *kids*—usually in their late teens or early twenties, an essential part of the seasonal workforce holding full- and part-time jobs in retail stores, restaurants, as lifeguards, beach workers, baby-sitters and anything else a hectic summer demanded. Some of them lived with their families, but the majority of them were out on their own, crammed together with a bunch of friends in one of the Island's many *animal houses*—those that because of location or condition were the least desirable to families and, naturally, more affordable. All three of these groups formed the lifeblood of the Island's economy, infusing enough money in taxes and consumer spending between Memorial Day and Labor Day to last all year.

*   *   *

Typical to most barrier islands, the eastern shore of the Reach is white sandy beach from tip to tip. Its irregular western bank, on the bay, has been almost entirely bulkheaded. Its width will vary from just three or four blocks in certain parts of the Island to as much as nine or ten blocks at other spots. Its main thoroughfare, the "Boulevard," runs the entire sixteen mile length of the Reach, through five separate boroughs, each being roughly three-plus miles long. Separately incorporated municipalities meant each borough had its own mayor, police force, local ordinances, building codes and unique personality, dictated in part by its inhabitants, taxes and prevailing power structure.

Farthest north was Dune City, the last and, consequently, the least developed part of the Island. Here was where the real money resided. Where even the most modest of homes far exceeded a million dollars in value. *Waterfronts*, whether on the ocean or the bay, started at three times that figure. There were few stores or businesses in Dune City and very little vehicular traffic and, except for a jogger here or there, practically no foot traffic. Occasionally one might drive up to see how far the area architects were pushing the envelope in design and construction when client money was no object. But aside from that, or a rare delivery vehicle, Dune City was very quiet, very secluded, very elite and virtually private.

South of Dune City was the borough of Cedar Terrace. More populated, it was a combination of older cottages, Cape Cods and the more recently designed contemporary homes built on pilings. Any new construction on the Reach, regardless of the borough, was required to be built on pilings to help minimize property damage during storms and high tides. Cedar Terrace was dotted with many of the Island's trendier shops and restaurants and the Boulevard was almost entirely commercial from this point south for a good ten miles.

Next came Bayberry, at the center of the Reach and, being the location of the causeway bridge to and from the mainland, naturally the most congested of the five boroughs. Bayberry's homes were much the same as in Cedar Terrace with a mixture of small and large, new and old. Bayberry had been the logical choice for construction of the causeway for many reasons. Not only was it at the midpoint of the Island, allowing equal access from both the north and south, it was also the widest part of the Reach with a natural, narrow peninsula jutting almost three quarters of a mile westward toward the mainland. And if that weren't enough, God had helped further by placing a series of tiny Islands, good for little else other than bridge supports, in a perfectly straight line and fairly evenly spaced continuing clear across to the opposite side of the bay.

Below Bayberry was South Beach, where all the action was. Home to most of the bars and clubs, miniature golf courses, the Island's only movie house and bowling alley, surf shops, fast food of every kind, ice cream parlors, a summer stock theater, most if not all of the Island's *animal houses* and a porn emporium that, while absolutely no one would admit to ever having set foot in, was the only establishment open twenty-four hours a day, all year long. South Beach also had Holiday Acres, a sprawling amusement park with adult and children's rides and a huge indoor game arcade that on a single rainy afternoon would take in more money than most middle class families earned in an entire year. Holiday Acres was where most summer residents would send their kids for their first work experience. It was almost mandatory that when you turned fifteen you applied for a part-time job there and no one was ever refused. Turnover was always high, partly because pay for minors was below minimum wage and their hours were restricted to twelve a week, but mostly because jobs like *ticket taker* or *change maker* just weren't very challenging, even for a fifteen-year-old. Most kids simply stopped showing up after a few weeks.

Finally, at the southern end of the Island was the borough of Cooper Point and at its tip stood Cooper Light, both named for one of the Island's earliest settlers, a Quaker family that arrived in 1808. The Cooper family, starting with its patriarch Joshua, played a major role in the development of Reach Island that has now spanned six generations. Joshua's grandson, Josiah Cooper, built the lighthouse in 1859, and served as its first keeper for four decades until his death in 1901, when his wife Jeanette, herself as strong as an ox, assumed his grueling duties and carried on for another twelve years. The majestic lighthouse, called "Old Coop" now by almost everyone, with its distinctive design of white lower half, cerulean blue upper half and yellow cupola, was a beacon of safety for ships traversing the Atlantic coastline for more than a century. Having been lit for the last time in 1963, it is now a national landmark and museum in the care of New Jersey's State Parks Commission and still the heart of the borough. Cooper Point looks quite different from the rest of the Reach. The oldest part of the Island, it carries its maturity with an air of genteel grace not found in the northern boroughs. Its streets are visibly wider and most of the homes are of the Victorian style with expansive columned shade porches and multi-gabled roofs.

Cooper Point is home to a goodly portion of the Island's permanent residents and business owners who never fail to breathe a sigh of relief every September; glad, so they say, to finally get the Island back all to themselves. Of course since all the money also leaves it's not too long before these same people are bemoaning the fact that there will be so many months before the hordes of summer vacationers return again.

J'net

I wonder if this is the last time I'll travel. Haven't traveled alone since I met Joe twelve years ago. Course, Belize is different to-

day. We'd notice little things each time we went back to visit Joe Jr. every year or so. Biggest change is the highway. It's finished now all the way down to Punta Gorda so I guess I can make it up to Belize City in a couple of hours by bus if I want. Or Joe Jr. can always drive down to the hut on weekends. If he wants. Course it's not really a hut. We just called it that cause it's kinda small. Has everything you need, really. But it's simple. Makes life seem real simple just bein' there. And that's okay with me. I like simple. The simpler the better. That's why I got rid of all those extra letters in my name. I didn't need em. J'net works fine for me. Joe says I'm the second with that name to marry into the Cooper family. The first was back in the eighteen hundreds. Tended the lighthouse all by herself I'm told. Anyway, I'm not sure why I picked Belize to go to way back then. Probably the rain forest and the jungle. And the Maya ruins. I guess I like learnin' about things. Now that I think about it, seems I did a lot of my travelin' between husbands. Especially after Vincent, my second. That trip to Finland to see the Northern Lights. That was a good one. And goin' down the Amazon by boat, stayin' in tree houses at night! Friends tellin' me to act my age. Well, I thought I was! Anyway, I certainly wasn't lookin' for another husband but, there I was on another trip to a place with a wild history, pirates and the like, sittin' on the rooftop cocktail terrace of a jungle lodge listenin' to the sounds of howler monkeys and sippin' my customary evenin' scotch and I look a little to my left and there was Joe Cooper, rugged and handsome as all get out, doin' exactly the same thing. Well, I'm not sure which one of us swept the other off their feet more but, to make a long story short, we enjoyed an evenin' scotch together just about every night for the next twelve years. Joe sure wasn't like most other men I'd known and not at all like my first two husbands. Same age as me, sixty-six. Not a talker, probably because of his Quaker heredity. And never a foul word of any kind. Strong, caring and as honest as they come. Joe tried to visit his son as often as he could since he moved down there several years earlier, and that's what he was doin' when we met. He introduced me to him three days later when we were back in Belize City where he was an assistant manager in a bank just before we had to head back to the States. Joe Jr. was thirty-one years old and real good lookin'. Too good lookin'. And he wasn't married and never would be givin' his particular set of circumstances. Course, he did have what's known as a "life mate" whose name, believe it or not, was also Joe! "Joe and Joe" as everybody referred to em. Funny how you never come across that with normal couples. I mean there's plenty names that both men and women can have. Like "Fran" or "Sam" or "Alex" or "Jackie" or even "Leslie." But you never run into that in a regular marriage. At least I never did. Anyway, the situation always pained Joe no end. Joe Sr. I mean. And not just because of the lifestyle thing though that must've been pretty hard to accept too, givin' his Quaker lineage and all. No, Joe would never stop lovin' his only son just because he couldn't condone or even understand the path he took in life. Blood's blood he'd always say. But Joe Jr. was the last of the Cooper male offspring and that meant the name would surely disappear on the Reach after two centuries of bein' such a vital part of it. Anyway, we had a nice visit with his son in Belize City and Joe convinced me to take a detour to the Reach before I went back to La Jolla, and he didn't exactly have to twist my arm. We had a wonderful little wedding not four weeks later. Joe and Joe came up for it. One of his rare trips back cause he knew that out of sight meant out of mind for the most part with friends and what few family members there were. He always felt the homosexual thing made people uncomfortable, especially his father. Like everybody knew but pretended not to. Except for his boyhood friend Kevin Flaherty. He was "Father" Kevin Flaherty now back at Saint Josephat's, the Island's only Catholic church, where he'd been an altar boy so many years ago. "Father Kev" to everyone who knew him today. Anyway, Joe's place on the Reach was a dream. His great uncle had built it back in the thirties and it was all cedar and mahogany inside and out with real intricate hand-carved woodwork through and through. Right on the bay in Bayberry and abutting an eight-house development called Bay Vista that Joe himself had just finished. All eight had recently been sold. Well, that's not really accurate. More like seven had been sold and one was stolen. Course, with Joe still havin' some Quaker attributes himself, namely not talkin' much about things that weren't pleasant, I didn't learn about that particular fact until many years later. And it was a real blow to Joe when it happened too, him bein' so honorable and then bein' railroaded like he was in such a shameful manner. Anyway, new people moved into all the houses at Bay Vista and a neighborly way of life sorta set in durin' the summer months. Well, I came to know all eight summer resident families on that little street over the next twelve years and I grew real fond of almost all of em. That's "Almost" with a capital A.

Three
No, the Fat One

"Hello."

"Put Joe on!"

"Oh my. Roland, is that you?"

"I'm sorry, J'net," he said, softening his voice. "Is Joe there? It's important."

"Sure, I'll get him. Hold the line." Cupping her hand over the receiver and calling out through the kitchen door, "Joe, it's Roland, says it's important."

Roland Oliveteen, and his father before him, had been the Coopers' attorneys for decades, handling all of the family's legal matters, both personal and business. The Oliveteen law firm enjoyed handsome fees from their ongoing relationship and the Coopers benefited from the exemplary service and advice they'd always received. Matters were handled smoothly, professionally and with a steady hand. Problems, which were few and usually small ones, were always solved quickly and relatively painlessly by Roland who, it seemed, never lost his easygoing, reassuring demeanor. So it was surprise, and more than a little alarm that registered in Joe when he put the receiver to his ear and listened as Roland spoke in a manner that was completely out of character.

"We need to talk!"

"Okay, Roland, what about?"

"Not over the phone! Your place, in an hour."

"Okay."

"Call Lars and Drew and Ben and tell them to be there too. *Especially* Ben, that horse's ass! And tell the stupid son-of-a-bitch to bring a fucking tape measure with him!"

"What?"

"One hour!" The line went dead.

Joe put the receiver down and sat there for a minute, stunned. He'd heard that Roland had a temper, but he never saw it displayed before. What could this be about? It had to have something to do with Bay Vista. That's the only project they were all involved with presently, he said to himself, so it would have to be Bay Vista. But that one's all but over now. The certificates of occupancy were due to come down any day now. The closings, all eight of them, were already tentatively scheduled. Starting next week. We would have heard about a problem from the building department, if one existed, a long time ago. *Tape measure?* What's *that* all about?

Joe started making the calls. Lars was a little annoyed, but said he'd be there. Drew was in a meeting, but his secretary said he was due out any moment and she would give him the message. It was almost two in the afternoon so Joe called the Jolly Roger, knowing he'd probably find Ben Bolen there and of course he was, already half in his cups. Ben's current workday rarely lasted more than a couple of hours and he'd start holding court at the local watering hole even before the lunch crowd began drifting in. Ben was always loudmouthed and often rude. So it was no surprise that he was more than a little pissed at being ordered to a meeting without being given any notice. Or even a reason, for that matter. Joe thought he could sense a little trepidation mixed in with his angry protests but he finally agreed to come.

He hung up and gazed across the street at his little Bay

Vista enclave, the houses now complete except for some final paint touch-up here and there, a few missing switch plates still to be mounted and, in number six, the upstairs carpeting and refrigerator due to be delivered and installed this week. Other than that all eight homes were ready to be turned over to their new owners a full month before the '82 season was to begin. What could be *wrong?* he kept asking himself while he waited for everyone to arrive.

* * *

The bay separating the Reach from the mainland had a well-marked channel which swerved this way and that its entire sixteen-mile length and was part of the eastern Intracoastal Water Waterway System going all the way down to Florida. The bay itself, except for the deep-water channel, was difficult to negotiate for anyone not familiar with its waters. Except for small boats with outboard motors and ones having very short drafts which could usually travel almost anywhere on the bay, one had to be extremely careful and often lucky not to run aground when venturing astray of the channel. The bay's vastness was deceiving to anyone but the most experienced boatmen. Water depth could vary from forty feet or more in some places to less than a foot in others at low tide without much warning. The myriad of sandbars to be found all over the bay were sometimes below the surface just enough not to be visible until it was too late. Added to this was the fact that the bottom of the bay was constantly shifting with strong currents, especially during the winter months. What was deep water today might not be next season. So the bay was always an adventure and, if your boat's draft was more than two feet, and you boasted that you never ran aground, you were probably lying.

Fronting the bay on the Island were homes its entire

length interrupted only infrequently by commercial enterprises—yacht clubs, marinas and a few waterfront restaurants. The best areas were those with deep water stretching from the property bulkhead all the way out to the channel. And the very best of these were those located in one of the Island's many natural coves which afforded some protection from the strongest north-south currents and usually meant that you were far enough away from the channel not to be bothered by the wakes that were generated by some of the larger boats passing by. One such area was Bay Vista.

Joe Cooper made the most of what was available to him in developing the Bay Vista property with an intelligent plot plan that provided for five bay-front homes and three more directly behind them, separated by a narrow private street. The plan took advantage of every inch of space on the all-important waterfront side, designing the largest homes possible while still maintaining the borough's minimum setbacks of twenty-two feet between dwellings and street boundaries. The three not directly on the water were situated so as to have a clear view of the bay and, almost as important, the magnificent sunsets the Reach was famous for. Sitting on any one of those three homes' west-facing decks, one could peer through the twenty-two feet of open space separating those on the bay and have a wonderful view. Not quite as expansive as the other five, of course, but still pretty wonderful all the same. That, plus the fact that the interior homes did not provide for the docking of a boat, was reflected in their selling price of $200,000 each, while the five directly on the bay went for $295,000. All eight houses were roughly the same size, with subtle design variations that made each unique and in total harmony with the others. They were two-story contemporaries, built on pilings high enough to walk under. Each had four bedrooms, two up and two down, two full baths, a kitchen, dining room, living room and a storage shed and outdoor shower under the house. There was new bulkheading on the bay and those five homes each had a new thirty-five foot dock right in their backyards. The development was sparsely landscaped, in keeping with the beach environment, and small, washed, white stones covered the entire property. The beach was only three blocks to the east. Highly desirable homes in a highly desirable location. All indications pointed to their selling in record time.

Joe, as the general contractor, usually worked with the same people he always had in the past, especially at the outset of his projects and this one would be no different. The funds for the acquisition of the property and building loans would be provided by Atlantic Bank, through his close friend Drew Wicker, who also happened to be its president. The Wicker family, themselves with Quaker heritage, dated almost as far back as the Coopers did on the Reach. Lars VanArsen would of course be the architect. Lars wasn't one of the outrageously expensive "brand-name" architects that worked exclusively up in Dune City, receiving virtual blank checks to let their imaginations run wild. Lars was talented, reliable, workmanlike, and remarkably creative, given the budget restraints he usually worked under. The project's property engineer and plot planner would again be Ben Bolen, though he'd increasingly been spending less and less time in his business and more and more of it in a bottle. There was a time when Ben was the only act in town at what he did, giving him a great deal of power. And he knew how to use it. As the site engineer he all but controlled when a project would get under way, often giving contractors fits. He'd sometimes delay a job for three or four weeks on a whim just because he could, and a lot longer if he thought you showed him less respect than he felt he deserved. Most people in the business made a real effort to stay on his good side. But other engineers were now working on the Island and Ben no longer wielded the power he once did. Competition wasn't something he handled well and these days he spent most of his time living on past glory. But Ben and Joe had a long history and, if nothing else, Joe was loyal. Sometimes to a fault. Joe had a hard-earned great reputation and always had his pick of sub-contractors in all of the building trades. They'd work for him before just about anyone else, because they knew they would always be paid on time, not such a common trait, with many GCs spread too thin, often biting off more than they could chew. As always, when the homes were ready, they'd be marketed by Drew's wife Bonnie through her real estate agency. And it went without saying that anything of a legal nature would rest in the hands of Roland Oliveteen.

As was usually the case with Joe's projects, everything worked pretty much as planned during the development of the Bay Vista property. Things played out like clockwork. Almost too good to be true in many respects. Cost estimates were right on target. No shortage of materials. The subs showed up on time, all the time. Even the weather cooperated with two milder than usual winters in a row that had little or no ill effect on any phase of construction. And all the homes did sell in record time, each one getting full asking price. Numbers one and two on the bay were snatched up by doctors from Philadelphia. Number three went to somebody in electronics. A CPA took number four. Number five on the bay was bought by an adman from New York. Number six across the street went to a lawyer, also from Philadelphia. In number seven was someone with a car dealership up north and, finally, number eight went to somebody who manufactured industrial wax of some kind.

Everything working out perfectly Joe thought, until an hour ago. But now something was very wrong. Something having to do with Ben Bolen and Roland was on his way over with whatever bad news it was.

*   *   *

Drew was the first to arrive, ten minutes early as was his custom, looking trim and dapper in charcoal slacks, crisp white shirt, navy tie with thin red horizontal stripes and his trademark spit-shined black wingtip shoes. Every bit the bank president, even without his jacket which he left in his car, and very overdressed for the Reach. But that was Drew. He gave J'net a hello and goodbye kiss, arriving just as she was on her way out, heading over to Saint Josephat's where she did volunteer work in their community center. Joe led Drew into the living room which was furnished with antiques and whose walls were almost all floor to ceiling bookshelves containing an organized clutter of Island crafts, artwork and bric-a-brac, collected over many decades.

"What's up?" Drew asked as he sank into one of the dark brown leather easy chairs.

"I don't know yet. But whatever it is it's not going to be good. Roland's on his way over and he's got some kind of bad news that he wouldn't talk about over the phone. Lars and Ben are coming too." They heard someone pull up onto the gravel driveway and, moments later, heard Lars bellowing his usual "*Let's level this tinder-box-junk-heap and put something pretty in its place!*" as the screen door slammed behind him. Lars lumbered into the living room and plopped into another easy chair, swinging a big, meaty leg over one of its arms. He grinned first at Drew and then at Joe and said "So, what's for dinner?"

It would be hard to find two people who were more different than Lars and Drew, certainly in their demeanor and personality, but especially in appearance. Drew polished, polite and always politically correct in any situation. Lars about as easy-going as a person could be; friendly, sloppy-looking and lovable. They both exuded a certain charm that was all their own and they both genuinely liked each other.

Lars was wearing an old tan tee shirt with recently acquired food stains on the front, worn denim cut-off shorts, unevenly frayed at about knee length, high-top black sneakers, unlaced as usual, grey sweat socks and a Yankees baseball cap.

Joe told Lars what he knew about the reason for their meeting, which wasn't much, and the three of them made small talk until the others arrived. Both Roland and Ben were usually late for appointments, though for very different reasons. Roland, try as he might to always leave his office on time, was invariably stopped by one or more of his staff with some question or urgent matter that couldn't wait for his return. Ben, on the other hand, was always purposely late in an effort to remind everyone, himself most of all, how very important he was. Today would be no exception, especially since he decided to have two more shots of bourbon chased by two more beers before he left the Jolly Roger.

Roland finally arrived and as he walked into the living room, he looked around and said "Where the hell is Bolen?" Before anyone could answer they heard Ben's truck pulling up outside on the gravel. All four men were seated around the room in silence when Ben walked in making sure his feet fell heavily and noisily on the wide-planked hardwood floor. He was pissed and he wanted everyone to know it.

"Somebody want to tell me what the hell this is about?" he said louder than was necessary, to no one in particular. It was obvious to everyone that Ben had just finished another liquid lunch.

"Sit your sorry ass down," came the reply, from Roland.

"What did you say?" Ben said, turning slowly to look at Roland. Everyone was looking at Roland. People didn't talk to Ben that way. It was usually the other way around. It was no secret that Roland never liked Ben, but still, he'd never shown hostility like this toward him before. In fact, not toward *anyone* that those present could think of.

"You heard me. Don't make me say it again." The two men stared at each other for a long moment, Ben trying to decide what to say next, a million thoughts running through his head. Roland's words and tone were more menacing than anything he'd heard directed at him in a long, long time. Hoping against hope, he kept telling himself they couldn't know. But what else could it be? He had a funny feeling about it when Joe first called him at the bar. It was always at the back of his mind, for almost two years now. But every day that passed meant that it was more and more unlikely that it would ever be discovered. *Stay cool*, he kept telling himself. *Maybe it's not what you think.* But deep down inside he knew better. He could almost feel his blood pressure rising. There were only two places left to sit. A stiff, uncomfortable looking straight-backed antique chair and the sofa, half of which was already occupied by Roland, whose relentless stare seemed to penetrate right into his suddenly throbbing head, reading his every thought. *Go for the chair,* he said to himself. And he did.

Roland cleared his throat, crossed his legs and began strumming his fingers on the arm of the sofa as he looked at the faces of the others around the room. Their expressions were all the same. A combination of bewilderment and anticipation, with a touch of fear of the unknown mixed in. Except for Ben, whose expression was one hundred percent pure dread. Perspiration started to form on his forehead and upper lip and dark splotches were visible on his shirt, at the armpits and chest. *Good*, thought Roland, *the biggest blowhard on the Island had finally lost his thunder*. He was in the hot seat and he was showing it.

"Gentlemen," he began, "I received a visit this morning from one of the buyers across the way," gesturing with his thumb toward Bay Vista. "He informed me that he was withdrawing his offer of $295,000 on the house and submitting a new offer of $100,000."

"What?" Joe said, not sure he heard right. "They're done deals. They're all in contract! The closings are imminent. You know that, Roland. He's gotta be nuts!" No one in the room had ever seen Joe show much emotion of any sort, so this was a little strange to see.

"He's not nuts, Joe," Roland continued. "He'd like us to void the contract and prepare a new one with his new terms."

"Tell him to go to hell," Joe said, now on his feet. Lars and Drew looked at each other not believing their ears. Joe actually said *hell*. This was really getting exciting.

"No, I don't think that would be the wisest thing to do," Roland said as calmly as possible, himself a little surprised to see Joe acting so *un*-calm. But this was bizarre news he was delivering to his friend. And it was going to get worse.

"Whoa, slow down a minute," Joe said, sitting down again. "Which one is it?"

"The Polack," replied Roland.

"Kosciusko?!?" Joe asked.

"No, the fat one."

"The fat one," Joe repeated, trying to put a name to the image in his head.

"Yes, the fat one."

"Meshitsky?"

"Meshitsky."

The others were in rapt attention. Lars had a somewhat amused look on his face. He didn't know the names of the new owners on Bay Vista, nor did he have reason to.

Drew was leaning forward rubbing his chin, a vague recollection of the name forming in his thoughts. He seemed to recall Bonnie mentioning it once or twice when she was involved in the sale of the homes a few months ago. He remembered her saying she didn't like one of the buyers and found him a little repulsive. And very fat.

Ben was straining to make sense of what he was hearing but his brain was operating on fewer than normal sober cells. The cacophony inside his head was getting louder by the minute. He couldn't make the scrambled pieces of his thinking come together in any way that made sense. Like looking at moving images through butter-smeared glass. Yet he knew that he should be able put two and two together. *"The fat one." "Meshitsky."* Something about it so close to making sense, but remaining just beyond his mental reach. *Meshitsky. Meshitsky. Fat.* Wait a minute. *Meshitsky. Brewsky. Fat. A brewsky for Meshitsky. How about another brewsky for Meshitsky.* Son-of-a-bitch, that's it! The fat guy at the bar last week.

Roland turned to look at Ben. The others followed suit. The anguish on his face was painful to see for everyone but Roland who just stared at him with venom in his eyes and a sneer of utter contempt on his lips. Roland got up and walked over to where Ben was sitting in obvious, uncharacteristic fear. At six-feet-four Roland was an imposing figure, made even more threatening by the look of pure hatred on his face. He hovered over him with clenched fists.

"Tell them what you did, you miserable piece of rat shit."

What followed was hard to watch and even harder to believe. Thirty minutes of Ben having a total breakdown right before their eyes, sobbing, shaking, stuttering, wringing his hands, until the entire story came out. Roland, scowling and standing over him the whole time. Joe sat completely motionless and expressionless, staring down at his folded hands as he listened. Lars and Drew were slack-jawed, looking alternately at everyone else and at each other, an occasional *holy shit* escaping from Lars. When he'd finally finished Ben sat with his head down, chin resting on his chest, wiping at his eyes with his finger tips, and at his nose with the back of his hand, unable to look anyone in the face. A broken man.

Joe still hadn't moved. Never taking his eyes off his hands, which remained folded in his lap, he spoke very slowly and barely loud enough for everyone to hear. "You fucking bastard. Get out of my fucking house. Now."

Ben didn't need to be told twice. In his haste to finally be allowed to leave he tripped on a throw rug and fell to his hands and knees. Roland lifted him by the shirt collar and propelled him, half crawling, half walking out of the room and out the back door. Roland returned and went to the liquor cabinet, opened it, took an unopened bottle of Cutty Sark and four shot glasses out and set them on the coffee table. They heard Ben's truck start up and leave as Roland poured the drinks. He handed one to Joe who downed it and said, "What the fuck do I do now?" Lars shot a quick glance over at Drew, and the look on his face told him he was thinking the same thing: *One fuck, two fuckings, one bastard and a hell, all in less than forty minutes!*

* * *

The four men spent the rest of the afternoon discussing options, which weren't many. And polishing off the rest of the scotch. What Ben had told them was almost beyond belief. He admitted to his first mistake, a stupid one that probably never would have happened had he been sober at the time, and went on to confess to the most ill-devised and senseless cover-up imaginable.

It had been decided at the outset that work would begin

on Bay Vista at the southern end of the dead-end street and then progress north to the rest of the development. In that way materials could be delivered to the farthest house first and, as each phase of construction was finished, work could begin on the next, then the next, and so forth until all eight homes on both sides of the street were methodically and efficiently completed. Ben, in his capacity of plot surveyor and engineer, would mark where each one of a home's many support pilings were to be located prior to their being driven deep into the ground. Once the pilings were in and the framing phase had begun, he would move on to the next house and repeat the process. It was something he'd done a thousand times before and something, he would boast to anybody who'd listen, that he could do blindfolded. What he *couldn't* do though, he would soon discover, was do it inebriated.

Ben was readying for his annual five-day junket to Las Vegas just as Bay Vista was due to get under way. Joe was begging him to at least get the first home's markings done before he left so the pile drivers wouldn't lose the whole week that he'd be gone. Ben said that he would but by that time he'd already started his descent into the depths of alcohol-driven self-grandeur, spending most afternoons patronizingly talking shop at the Jolly Roger's huge racetrack-shaped bar, a favorite lunchtime destination with construction tradesmen. Ben's problem was that he rarely ate lunch and usually lingered long past the lunch hour, often striking up increasingly slurred conversations on almost any subject with anyone in his immediate proximity. On some days he would find himself sitting alone, long after the lunch crowd had left with no one being quite close enough to talk to without shouting. And it was on just such an afternoon two days before his trip that Ben, feeling a maudlin guilt about not yet keeping his promise, decided to go to the Bay Vista jobsite to set the pile markings on Joe's first house. His condition being what it was, the afternoon seemed to fly by. He worked feverishly that day, sinking pointed wooden stakes into the soft ground, attaching strings which he then stretched in perfectly straight lines to form the home's footprint. He then stretched more string, crisscrossed at right angles within the footprint to create a guide-grid for the pilings. He worked until sunset and decided it was too dark to continue. He'd completed most of the work. The rest could be finished in no time at all in the morning. Right now it was happy hour!

Ben returned late the next morning to finish. He checked all the measurements of the footprint for accuracy. Perfect. He then began attaching pieces of red tape to the intersecting strings at exactly the right spots, which would indicate placement of the pilings. He studied Lars' pile plan drawings and re-measured his tape markings to make sure every one was perfectly placed. Then he double-checked them again just to be sure. He didn't want anybody interrupting his vacation with problems. Finally satisfied that he had done his usual superlative job, he congratulated himself, got in his truck and headed for the Jolly Roger. He was thirsty. And hungry for a change. Today, he said to himself, he might even have lunch. By this time tomorrow, he was thinking, he'd be halfway to Vegas for some serious, well-earned good times.

When Ben returned from Vegas a week later there was a message from Joe saying that he could start marking the second lot. He planned to do just that the next morning but the hangover he had from all the free booze on the first class flight from Vegas the night before was now conspiring with a monster case of jet lag to keep him in bed until early afternoon. By the time he showered and had enough coffee to see straight it was past three in the afternoon. He decided to stop at the jobsite before hitting the bar for happy hour. It was almost four when he got there and the framers were beginning to pack up their tools and call it quits for the day. All the pilings were in and had been cut, and most of them already had the girders in place that would support the house above. Ben joined Fritz, the crew chief, who was leaning over a make-shift table made of saw horses and a six by eight foot section of plywood, where he was busy making notes on a set of Lars' construction plans. Ben glad-handed him, asking how everything was going. "No problems, as always," Fritz said, though Ben didn't really need an answer. Eyeballing the progress so far told him that, once again, his flawless markings resulted in a perfect interpretation of Lars' piling plan. Yet, the more he looked, the more uneasy he became. Something wasn't quite right but he couldn't put his finger on it. He studied the pilings and the girders. They looked right. They matched the plans. His eyes kept drifting to the south side of what would be the house. No one possessed as trained an eye as Ben. Thirty years in the business had taught him to see things that others simply couldn't. He knew that Fritz was speaking but he wasn't able to hear, or even care about what it was about, his attention now fully turned to the south pilings and the property boundary beyond. He did not like what he was seeing and his first inkling, or more accurately, his *hope,* was that Fritz and his crew had screwed up. But as he gazed around at all the pilings he knew that that wasn't the case. Almost all of the strings, with their red tapes still attached, remained stretched between the stakes exactly as he'd left them a week ago. No, if there *was* a fuck-up, which he was now sure there was, it was his and his alone. The sickening feeling in the pit of his stomach told him in no uncertain terms that that was the case. He tried as best as he could to mask his mounting fear as he waited for Fritz and the others to leave. As soon as they had he went to his truck to get a tape measure and walked to the south property boundary and laid it out on the ground between it and the nearest piling.

"*Shit!*" was all he could say.

*   *   *

The regulars at the Jolly Roger wondered to themselves what was wrong with Ben, never having seen him acting as he did later that day. Knowing he had just returned from Las Vegas, they just chalked it up to him probably dropping a bundle while he was out there, and left it at that. To a man, they were glad not to hear his condescending blabber for a change, and no one really cared much that he sat drinking alone, deep in troubling thought and looking about as morose as a person could.

Ben spent the first hour at the bar that day trying to figure out what happened. The plot plan called for the house to be twenty-two feet from the property line but he could tell that it wasn't as soon as he gave it a good look. Measuring confirmed that there was twenty-*six* feet between the two points, four feet more than there was supposed to be. That in itself wasn't a problem. The problem was the remainder of the property, which was planned out with hardly an inch to spare. After a while he stopped thinking about *how* it happened because he just couldn't find an answer. He refused to blame it on the alcohol he'd consumed that day before he started working. After all, he told himself, the rest of the job was done perfectly, wasn't it? So it couldn't be that. But he *had* screwed up. Of that there was no doubt and nothing could change that fact. The problem at hand was what to do about it now.

He ordered another drink, his fourth since he'd arrived, and outlined the possibilities in his head. He could fess up. Start over four feet to the south. A few thousand dollars worth of pilings and timber wasted. And a few days' labor on the part of the framers and pile drivers. Costly, but doable, even if he had to foot the bill for most of it himself. Or more likely, all of it. Still, he could handle it financially. But could he handle it on a professional level? He looked around the bar at the people he knew there. It could never be kept a secret. His reputation would be shot to hell and his prestige a thing of the past. No, he wouldn't let that happen. He could come clean to Joe and implore him to build the other four houses a foot shorter in width. But you can't just lop a foot off each house. It would entail Lars knowing about it too, and he'd have to go back and redesign each one, top to bottom, inside and out. It would take months and they'd have to start the whole approval process all over again with the building department. Way too costly in time. Not to mention the debt service on all the money Joe was already into the bank for. Plus there was no guarantee that word wouldn't get out. Lars might leak it. Accidentally or even purposely. You could never be sure about people. Plus someone in the building department might figure it out. He would still end up being the laughing stock of the Island. Not a good idea.

He ordered another drink. The more he thought about it the more he knew what he had to do. All things considered, it was probably the only way to go.

Someone at the end of the bar bought him another drink. By the time he finished it he'd made up his mind.

* * *

Roland was saying what none of the others wanted to hear, especially Joe. It had become apparent after much discussion that Mr. Meshitsky indeed had them by the short curlies and they had no choice but to acquiesce to his outrageous demands.

Ben's problem, and in turn their problem too, started because he was a lush. And though he almost got away with his bone-headed plan at a cover-up, being a lush was what finally did him in again. In fact, had he not had the misfortune of being seated on a barstool in the wrong place, at the wrong time, in the wrong condition, next to the wrong man, he might have actually pulled it off without ever having been found out.

What Ben decided to do seemed simple enough. Risky, but not as much as the other ideas he had rejected as being definitely and totally ruinous. He knew that four feet too few would be as easy to spot as four feet too many, as he himself had done earlier at the jobsite. This would be especially true if it was located at the northern, curb-end of the development. Eighteen feet where there was supposed to be twenty-two was sure to be discovered by borough inspectors if he allowed the project to progress as planned. But, he theorized, having one less foot *between* the five houses would have a much better chance of going undetected. Probably never even checked . The design of the homes, having several different plains along their sides would actually play into the scheme and help. Having twenty-one feet between the houses instead of twenty-two would not be easy to discern, even by someone with as trained an eye as he had. So that would be the plan. The four lost feet would be regained by taking one foot from each of the spaces separating the five bay-front homes. To make it even more difficult to discover he would do the same thing across the street between the other three. And that was the plan he put into motion, starting the very next day.

* * *

When Ben was drunk it was easy for him to *really believe* that he had outsmarted everyone. Those were the only times he felt safe with his long-harbored secret. His fear dissipated. As did the realization that he had done anything wrong in the first place. Fear and reality were replaced with indignant superiority, and he said things that he shouldn't, having no concern whatsoever of the consequences. When drunk, he became *all-powerful* and *untouchable* by those he deemed inferior, which pretty much included everyone.

It was during one of these times that Lloyd Meshitsky, about to become the proud owner of a brand new home at Bay Vista, which he'd just left after taking some room measurements, happened to stop in the Jolly Roger for a cold one. It being late afternoon and not yet happy hour, Ben was all alone at the big bar. He was also drunker than he'd ever been before. Lloyd scanned the room thinking he might as well start meeting some of the locals and, seeing Ben, headed toward him. Pulling up a stool which was far too inadequate for his considerable ass, he hoisted himself onto it and immediately felt it start to give, hearing faint cracking sounds. He quickly got off, deciding it more prudent to stand and pushed the stool off to the side, knowing full well that the next person who tried to sit on it would end up on the floor.

The bartender walked over and Lloyd thrust a puffy, sweaty hand across the bar at him, saying "Lloyd Meshitsky, CPA. Good to meet you." The bartender, having little choice, shook hands while an immediate dislike began to register. He'd seen this type before. He retracted his hand as quickly as he could, wiping it on a bar towel with a bit more vigor than was really necessary, and just waited in silence for the stranger to order, already having decided that politeness wasn't too important in this instance. Lloyd continued, saying "My good man, Meshitsky needs a brewsky, the coldest one you have." Lloyd looked at Ben slouching in the seat next to him and added "And bring a brewsky for my new friend here as well!" He turned to face Ben, extended his hand again, flashed a big toothy smile and said "Lloyd Meshitsky, CPA. Pleasure to meet you."

* * *

"Can you believe it?" Roland was saying. "The stupid son-of-a-bitch must've been drunk out of his mind. He told Meshitsky everything. Or at least enough for him to do some sniffing around on his own. Found out all he needed to, I guess. He knows he's got us over a barrel."

They *were* over a barrel. Well, at least Joe was. That was for sure. And, to a lesser extent Drew was too, with his bank already into the project to the tune of almost two million dollars. As far as Lars was concerned he wasn't sure why Roland even wanted him to be there in the first place. Probably to lend a little moral support to Joe. And that was fine with him. Joe was a decent guy and he certainly didn't deserve this.

They had gone over the situation from every angle all afternoon and were now resigned to the fact that Meshitsky would be getting his way. Had this mess happened a couple of years earlier it probably wouldn't be such a problem. Back then the powers that be weren't sticklers to detail like they are today. Plus, everybody in the room had a little clout with the folks in charge in those days. More often than not they could be persuaded to look the other way with something as trivial as this. And if that didn't work Roland would somehow always find a way to successfully obtain a zoning variance and make the problem go away. But that was then and this was now. A new mayor was in office and, with him, a new administration. They were voted in on a promise of running a tighter ship and spent the last three years doing just that. They had literally cleaned house, ridding the borough of the old line, mid and lower level bureaucrats. The mayor was particularly hell-bent on making sure that the zoning and building departments dotted the i's and crossed the t's and toed the line in every respect. Everyone knew it, especially the four men in Joe's living room that day. They also knew that the mayor would absolutely *feast* on this situation if he ever got wind of it. He would like nothing better than to make an example of someone, especially someone with a time-honored name like Cooper. Making Joe bulldoze the whole development and start over and levying hefty fines to boot would be the likely scenario. Joe would be ruined.

"I'm afraid you're gonna have to bite the bullet, Joe," Roland was saying.

"And eat two hundred grand," Joe replied.

"Yes, and eat two hundred grand. I don't see any other way, do you?"

No one said a word. There was nothing to say. Roland continued on. "I'll tell the bastard you've agreed and prepare a new contract."

"Well, I guess that's it," Drew said, starting to get up from his chair.

"Hold on a sec, Drew. There are a couple of other things we need to discuss." Drew sat back again and looked at Roland with a quizzical expression on his face. "It seems Mr. Meshitsky has two more requests as part of the deal."

"Yes? And they are?"

"He has decided not to put any money down on the purchase and he would like us, meaning in this case *you*, to arrange for a fifteen-year, interest-only mortgage with a balloon payment of the full principle at the end of the term."

"Interest-only? No money down? I've never heard of such a thing!" Drew said.

"He says it's a thing of the future. He says you'll be ahead of your time."

Drew rubbed his chin, looking more than a little perplexed. "I'm almost afraid to ask . . . at what rate would he like this loan?"

"A half of one percent."

Drew burst out laughing. "This is a joke, right? Tell me you're joking."

"I'm not joking, Drew. And neither is he, I'm afraid."

"How the hell can I do that? I've got a board of directors to contend with, in case you didn't know!"

"It's not a lot of money, Drew. You can figure a way."

Drew sat thinking and shaking his head, like he needed to clear it of cobwebs. The room was silent for a minute or two, all eyes now on Drew.

Joe said to Roland, "This isn't Drew's problem. I'll hold a private mortgage."

"No, it's okay, Joe," Drew said. "I think I'll be able to work something out. I can set it up in a way that won't be scrutinized. I'm pretty sure I can do it."

Roland nodded at Drew, as if to say thanks and turned his attention to Lars, who hadn't said a word in some time. Lars looked around the room, smiling broadly at everyone and said to Roland, "Okay Rol, I knew there had to be a reason you invited me to this swell party. Lay it on me."

"Don't worry, Lars. This'll be pretty painless. Mr. Meshitsky would like some alterations made on the second floor, and we need you to just make sure it's structurally safe. And prepare any drawings that might be needed."

"Uh huh. And the alterations he wants?" Lars said, still smiling, waiting for more.

"He wants to eliminate the second bedroom up there and make the whole thing one big room. Says he's only got two kids and there are already two bedrooms downstairs for them."

"I guess he doesn't plan on having many houseguests," Lars said. "No big deal. Anything else?"

"Yes. He also wants a Jacuzzi installed in the middle of the room."

"A Jacuzzi in the middle of the room."

"Yes. Jumbo."

"Did you say jumbo?"

"Yes. A jumbo Jacuzzi. In the middle of the room."

"And how jumbo should this jumbo Jacuzzi be? The one in the middle of the room."

"As jumbo as jumbo Jacuzzis come."

"Okay, got it. Consider it done. Now, who do I bill? Just kidding! Just kidding!" he said, smiling and throwing his hands up in front of his face, feigning to fend off the scowl he got from Roland. "Just give me forty-eight hours and it'll be done."

After a long silence, Roland said that that was all he had, adding, "As if that weren't enough."

"Enough for one day, that's for sure," agreed Drew, thankful that it *was* all he had.

Joe just sat quietly, shaking his head at times, still not wanting to believe this day had really happened.

Drew wanted to say something, anything, to help his friend who, in a matter of a few hours, had lost every nickel of profit in a project he'd been working on for more than two years.

"Make him pay, Joe. Make Ben pay you back, even if the piece of scum has to work for free for the next hundred years!" Joe just looked at him, gave him a little nod and smiled sadly, as if there was a chance in hell he would ever let Ben work for him again.

"You want to know what the worst part is?" Joe asked the

room in general. "What bothers me the most? Meshitsky'll be living right across the way. Every summer. I'll have to see him on a daily basis." He looked out the window toward Bay Vista, the sun setting now, and then turned to face Roland. "The man is a pig, Roland."

"That he is, Joe. That he surely is."

They heard a car pulling into the driveway. It was J'net returning from her volunteer work. Roland looked at his watch and, seeing that it was already six-thirty, said, "Let's call it a day."

"Amen," Lars said. Then, in an attempt to lighten the gloom permeating the room, added, "So, what's for dinner?" It got a laugh from everyone, even a tiny one from Joe.

J'net walked in and said, "My, this must be an important meeting." They all lingered a while in the living room exchanging pleasantries with J'net, trying not to let on that anything was wrong.

After a few minutes Roland looked at his watch again and said it was time to leave. J'net protested, saying they must stay for dinner, adding "It's my garlicky chicken tonight!" They made their apologies, saying they wished they could but that they really had to go. Even Lars, who went absolutely gaga over anything garlic and was sorely tempted to accept the offer, thought it wiser to leave. They said their good-byes and made their way out.

Later that night, after a dinner that Joe barely picked at in silence, J'net watched with some concern as he went to his tool cupboard and fished around until he found what he was looking for. Without a word, he walked out and across to Bay Vista with a flashlight and tape measure. He returned ten minutes later, tossed them back into the closet, and, for the first time since they were married, silently went off to bed without so much as a *goodnight.*

Joe didn't enjoy a truly restful night's sleep the rest of

his life. They were invariably punctuated with more than a normal amount of tossing and turning, periods of insomnia and a great deal of mumbling. If J'net was awake on those nights, she would try to make out what Joe was saying but, except for clearly hearing him utter an occasional "*pig,*" it was completely unintelligible.

J'net

I didn't find out what really happened until after the funeral. Drew and Bonnie told me the whole story one day when they were visitin'. Course, I surmised it had somethin' to do with Ben Bolen who abruptly disappeared from all conversation and involvement in Joe's affairs. Like he never even existed. After a while Joe pretty much returned to bein' almost normal. For him, that is. His sleep was always a little fitful though, even on his good days. Course, he was a quiet man way before whatever happened actually happened. So his bein' a little extra quiet at times wasn't that much out of character. Fairly normal to people that didn't know him like I did. But then there were times when he'd suddenly go completely catatonic on me all over again. Might last a day. Might last longer. But he'd always come out of it. Gradually though. It took me years, maybe about four or five, before I noticed a connection. At first it seemed that hot weather had somethin' to do with his moods. Like he was in a bad way much more often durin' the summer season. But it wasn't the heat. There were many days when it was hotter'n hell and he'd be just fine. Then one day somethin' happened that couldn't be ignored. Joe was in the front yard busy puttin' a new screen on one of the windows. I was in the side yard doin' some gardenin'. Lloyd Meshitsky and his wife, Shirley, were walkin' their dog. A real nice Golden Retriever named Barney, as tame and docile a dog as ever there was, except for some reason when Shirley tried walkin' him all by herself. That dog went out of control when he was alone with her.

Like a Jekyll and Hyde dog. Bad with Shirley, good with everybody else. And though it always turned out exactly the same, Shirley would still try walkin' him alone. She just refused to ever learn her lesson. It was always real comical for anyone watchin'. The dog nearly yankin' her arm out of its socket, pullin' her this way and that, draggin' her faster than she ever knew she could run, her free arm flailin' and grabbin' at air, and all the time her pleadin' with him to "Heel Barney goddammit heel Barney heel!" Until it ended the way it always did, with her screamin' at the top of her lungs for help, "Oh shit. Lloyd! Oh shit. Lloyd!" And time after time big fat Lloyd would have to come rescue her. Anyway, there we were in the yard tendin' to our chores and the Meshitskys are walkin' by with the dog nice and calm cause Lloyd's got hold of the leash and Lloyd hollers over to Joe "Hey, neighbor, how's it hangin' old buddy?" Now Joe, who had his back to them, dropped the screen like it was on fire and literally froze stiffer than a statue and I swear I could see the hair on the back of his neck bristlin'. He stood there, kinda motionless for a good minute and then just walked into the house and went comatose on me again for the next two days. Course, by then it was no secret that the Meshitskys had a knack for rubbin' people the wrong way. Not the daughter so much, she was pretty harmless. And Shirley I guess was sorta tolerable, though just barely, mainly because of her intellect bein' in kinda short supply. Tedious just talkin' to her at times. Lloyd, though, and that damn son of theirs were another story altogether. Most people would say they weren't likable from the minute they met em. And their odiousness seemed to have a life of its own, increasing with every encounter. Anyway, I don't know why I didn't put two and two together sooner. Guess I just thought Joe had a dislike for that family a little more than most other people did. Before the incident in the yard that is. That's when I started pressin' Joe to tell me what it was about. All he was ever willing to say on the subject though was that he'd been seriously wronged by the man and there was nothin' to do about it but wait till the Good Lord saw fit to rightly serve him his just deserts. He'd often say that the Reach had a way of dealin' with people like that and metin' out its own brand of justice. "Island justice" he liked to call it. Well, nothin's ever perfect they say and that was true for our little neighborhood too. One bad family in the mix can take its toll over time. And, over time, the Meshitskys, mainly Lloyd, found ways to seriously wrong just about everyone on Bay Vista and God only knows how many others as well. And the little bastard son wasn't any better and that's the truth. But we really did luck out with the rest of the folks though. Could never even have asked for a better bunch of people, that's for sure. My, if ever I was asked which of em I liked best I don't know if I'd be able to answer. They're wonderful families, all of em really. Course, I knew some better than others so naturally, in that small way, I kinda did have my favorites among em, but that's not to say the others weren't just as good. The ones I knew best were those on the bay, closest to us. The DiMarco family, right across the street. Nicest people you'd ever want to meet. The Meshitskys were next to them but we'll just skip over them and wish they didn't even exist. Then came the Kosciusko family and my, they certainly were pips! Next in line were the Gorshins and then the Drakes, both as grand as they come. The three families behind them, as far as I could tell were good people too, though as I said I didn't know them quite as well as the others, my main contact with them bein' at the season-endin' block party every year. They went by the names of Pearlstein, Mullin and Elias. Bottom line, those seven families were so nice they nearly nullified the badness of the other one. That's "Nearly" with a capital N.

Four
No Keisters

Lee Jack Kosciusko was a manufacturer's representative for many of the country's largest electronics companies. He traveled extensively in his job, which was to make sure that his lines of merchandise were sold-in to the various retail accounts, both large and small, that he had developed relationships with over the years. He made sure the latest new products were always in stock and well promoted by his accounts and that store personnel were adequately versed in the features and benefits of each product. Lee Jack was a natural-born salesman with a personality that made him extraordinarily successful. He liked his job, the travel it afforded him and greeted most of the world around him with a genuine smile. He liked his customers and they liked him right back.

He had been sitting in the passenger area of Delta Airlines' Gate 7 at Newark Airport waiting to board his flight for well over an hour. An announcement had just been made that the plane that would take him to Las Vegas had finally arrived on its prior leg from Atlanta, which meant at least another hour before take-off. *Jacko*, his nickname since college, disliked flight delays as much as anyone but probably for different reasons. Jacko just loved to fly and delays simply meant he'd have to wait that much longer before being airborne. When asked why he enjoyed it so much he would always explain, and only half-joking thought some who knew him, that he was from another planet and being thirty thousand feet above earth made him feel closer to home. His former wife, probably the only person in the world who didn't like him, may have actually believed it and listed his being an alien as one of the grounds in her divorce action. Jacko, his sense of humor never failing him, decided that among all the grounds listed in the suit this would be the only one he would not contest. He instructed his lawyer to try to have the divorce granted based on his being a visitor from the planet *Gorgon Zola*. Either the judge also had a good sense of humor or his caseload was too great for him to notice the gag, because when the divorce judgment finally came through it referred to the defendant, one Lee Jack Kosciusko, as indeed being from outer space.

Jacko kept a copy of the divorce decree handy at all times. Should anyone ever be skeptical about his story of originally touching down on a coastal hillside in Italy two centuries ago, carrying with him as a gift for those in his new world a wheel of his planet's strong smelly cheese, he'd just whip it out as undeniable truth. He would go on to explain that the little Italian province quickly embraced the cheese as its own and continues to this day to produce the powerful, aromatic blue-veined delicacy according to his original recipe. He would also proudly inform the listener that he of course named the cheese, and the little town that now makes it, after his all but forgotten former planet.

The story was always a great ice breaker, especially on airline flights. Even the grouchiest of people would quickly warm to Jacko's genuine friendliness and the story never failed to take unexpected twists and turns depending on the other person's ability to join in the banter.

Being from outer space though was the last thing anyone thought of when they saw Jacko for the first time. What they thought, without exception, was that he was Lee Trevino. Jacko didn't just *resemble* the famous golf pro, he was *his double,* and people seemed to either disregard or not notice at all the fact that Jacko was probably a good ten years younger than Trevino. That's how uncanny the similarities were. So it was totally understandable that Sharon Mahoney, also waiting to board the flight to Vegas and seated right across from Jacko in the gate area, was convinced that he was the colorful celebrity.

Sharon was the public relations director of Jutsi Electronics of North America, a relative newcomer in this country and a company that had yet to gain any degree of prominence in the crowded field of home entertainment marketers. While giants like Sony and Panasonic had become household names, selling billions of dollars worth of equipment, it was generally unknown that it was her little company, back in Japan, that had actually developed most of the technology that was at the heart of today's most popular products. No longer content in that obscure role, the company had recently decided to begin manufacturing and marketing its own line of branded merchandise and Sharon was hired to help get the word out. And that was the reason she was on her way to Las Vegas. The annual Consumer Electronics Show was the largest trade show in the industry and it was held there each year during the first week in July. This 1977 show, scheduled to begin in two days, was the setting Jutsi chose to introduce some of their newest and most exciting products, many having truly breakthrough technology that could set the pace for the entire industry in the coming years.

Sharon stared across at Jacko and, as she did, it became crystal clear that sitting there not ten feet away was the possible solution to her problem. Her company's top management, all recently arrived from Japan, was brilliant when it came to research and development, and that area of the company was always flush with all the money and attention it needed to continually push the envelope with new innovations. However, they were novices in the area of consumer marketing and, as yet, unwilling to make the financial commitment necessary to have any real impact. So, as Sharon continued to look at Jacko, thinking she was looking at Lee Trevino, she also saw an end to her frustration. If she had learned anything during the year and a half that she worked at Jutsi it was that the Japanese had a passion for three things: Technology, technology, and golf. And not necessarily in that order. They were absolutely gaga over golf and anything remotely related to it. So, naturally, her PR-savvy brain was fast formulating a plan of action. What would happen, she wondered, if she could persuade the great golf legend to stop by her company's booth? At bare minimum, the stir it would create would be the talk of the show and her bosses would be beside themselves with sheer delirium. And maybe, just maybe, she could make them see the possibilities of some sort of celebrity endorsement deal being explored. She could almost see them now, scurrying around to find the money for a real marketing effort. And find it they would. She was sure of it.

Sharon noticed that Jacko had tucked his boarding pass into the breast pocket of his jacket and his seat assignment, which had been scrawled with a black marker by the gate attendant, was clearly visible: 3-A. *Damn!* Sharon said to herself. *Of course he travels first class! Well, if she pulled this coup off she'd have no problem getting reimbursed for a measly upgrade. Assuming, of course, there were seats still available in the front cabin.* She looked around the waiting area and determined the 747 they'd be flying would only be about half full so there was a chance. She got up and walked toward the gate attendant and, as she did, attracted everyone's attention, including

Jacko's. Sharon was an absolutely stunning woman whose simplest of movements, like that of walking across a room, never failed to have that effect on people. This was 1977 so it would be quite some time before people would start telling her that she resembled someone destined to make male hearts skip a beat in years to come. She didn't know it then but Sharon Mahoney was the spitting image of the yet-to-be-discovered, incredibly beautiful actress Sharon Stone.

When she got to the gate attendant's desk she asked if there were any seats left in first class and was told there was one still available. Sharon said she wanted an upgrade and handed him her credit card. The man quickly made the adjustments.

"Seat 3-C, miss," he said handing her a new ticket and boarding pass.

"Do you happen to know who is in 3-B?" she asked him.

"Let's see," he said scanning the manifest in front of him. "That would be Mrs. Bean. I believe that's her over there," he continued, pointing to a tiny and somewhat prim looking lady perhaps in her early sixties, no doubt on her way to a lascivious rendezvous with a tall, dark and handsome slot machine. "Thank you," Sharon said and walked over to where the lady was seated.

"Excuse me, ma'am," Sharon began, "I wonder if you might do a tremendous favor for me," and within moments they had exchanged seats. "Thank you so much," she said and returned to her seat clutching the boarding pass that would put her next to Jacko for the five-hour flight.

* * *

As soon as they were on board and seated, he at the window and she on the aisle, Jacko gave her a big smile, extended his hand and said "Hi, I'm Lee" and before he could continue, Sharon, returning the smile, said "I know" and firmly took his hand, pumping it a few seconds longer than was necessary.

"I'm Lee," he repeated, "but everyone calls me Jacko. I'm from outer space."

"Hello, Jacko," she replied, wondering why she'd never heard he had a nickname. "My name's Sharon, but everyone calls me Spike. From New Brunswick," she added.

"Spike. That's excellent!" he said, looking into her eyes and deciding that wasn't the only thing that was excellent about her. She studied his smiling face for a long moment and was surprised to feel such an immediate and extraordinarily strong attraction toward him. They both realized they were still holding each other's hands and slowly, ever so reluctantly released them, each wondering why they didn't feel the embarrassment that should accompany such a prolonged hand embrace between perfect strangers. They settled back into comfortable first class leather seats and privately shared the same thought: *This might turn into a very interesting flight.* But neither of them could possibly have had a hint at just how interesting it would actually get.

As it turned out, Sharon and Lee, *Spike* and *Jacko,* had a great deal in common although it would be a couple of days before they would learn about much of it. For starters, they both bore a remarkable likeness to famous people, even though it would take some years for Spike's double to gain her notoriety. And, as if that wasn't enough, they both had the same first names as those of their respective celebrities. They both attended the same school, Rutgers University, although Jacko, being four years older, graduated just prior to Spike entering as a freshman. They also both got their nicknames there while playing varsity sports. Jacko had two impressive football seasons as a tailback, setting the school record for number of carries and finished just shy of breaking the record for yards gained. Since *Lee Jack Kosciusko* couldn't quite cut it as a catchy chant the student faithful simply did the required surgery to make it one. A cry of *Jacko! Jacko!* would reverberate throughout the stands every time he touched the ball. Sharon's experience was much the same. A natural athlete with great ability, she quickly made her mark on the volleyball team and, at a height of five-feet-ten-inches, immediately became the *go to* player for her extraordinary skill at spiking the ball at the net. With her amazing looks and rare talent it didn't take long for *Spike* Mahoney to become an instantly recognizable figure everywhere on campus.

All of these coincidences would eventually come to light but there was one thing they had in common that they would learn about almost immediately after take-off. Spike and Jacko shared a love for good food. They practically *lived* for it. They loved eating it. They loved cooking it. They loved entertaining and serving it to guests. They loved learning new dishes. They even had subscriptions to the same gourmet magazines. They were true *foodies* in every sense of the word, and that's the first thing they learned about each other on that fateful flight to Sin City.

It was also their custom to never eat airline meals, not even in first class where it was usually only marginally better. So it was no surprise that when the flight attendant came to take their order they both politely declined. While the airline's food held no interest for them Jacko knew that they often poured a decent caliber of wines in first class and he informed their cabin attendant that they would be partaking of them. She asked if they preferred white or red and Jacko, smiling broadly, simply answered "Yes." She asked again, this time receiving from Jacko a response of "Yes indeed." Spike intervened, explaining that he meant they would be having both. Jacko, addressing the attendant again, began a lengthy dissertation on the integrity of the grape and expectations of the vintner, weaving a story that may or may not have had anything to do with wine, and abundantly punctuated with a hodgepodge of superlatives and seemingly unrelated words and phrases. Seeing the helpless look on the face of the stewardess, Spike, who was surprised at actually understanding what Jacko was getting at, came to her rescue again saying, "He's just asking for four glasses." She hurried off and returned moments later with a tray on which were two freshly opened bottles of wine and four appropriately shaped stemmed glasses, two for white and two for red. Jacko examined the wines, a '72 Bethel Heights Pinot Noir and a '74 Alban Roussanne, both of which brought an approving smile to his face. Seeing it, and not wanting to risk another oration, she said, "Why don't I just leave them in your trustworthy care," and, scurrying off, added, "There's more where that came from!"

Jacko and Spike soon became immersed in conversation recalling memorable dishes and great restaurant experiences they'd had over the years. It wasn't long before they were boasting of their own accomplishments in the kitchen and describing their favorites with complete, unadulterated passion. They'd take turns, speaking in hushed tones, one of them explaining the dish and its preparation while the other would visualize it, often making sounds that bordered on sheer ecstasy. The combination of the wines and the descriptions of mouth-watering culinary delights that were sprouting from their lips like a hot-spring geyser had begun to affect them both like an aphrodisiac, especially Spike. It went on for over an hour. Mrs. Bean, sitting across the aisle, strained to hear what was being said but all she could really comprehend were the moans and groans emanating from whichever of the two happened to be the listener at the moment. Spike had just finished imparting her *Broiled bacon-basted veal tournedos with mushroom-oyster sauce*. Jacko was seeing it in his mind's eye and practically tasting it, abundant sounds of approval competing with the drone of jet engines. Spike tapped him on the leg and said "Your turn, big guy. Top that!"

Jacko thought a moment then embarked on a sensuous recital of his *Savory zuppa di pesce with cappacola and andouille sausage*. He had just finished listing the ingredients and was starting to heat the olive oil in a sauté pan when Spike suddenly stopped him, digging her fingernails into his thigh.

"Jacko, wait," she whispered hotly into his ear. "Want to join the *Mile-High Club*?" Jacko went silent, staring straight ahead, wide-eyed and blinking emphatically, not believing he actually heard what he thought he heard.

"Of course you do," she continued. "Listen to me, Jacko," her lips now lightly brushing his ear as she spoke. "I'm going to get up and go into that bathroom over there. I want you to wait two minutes and then walk to the door and, when you're sure no one's looking, knock very lightly three times. Have you got that, Jacko?"

Jacko only stared straight ahead, completely bug-eyed now, his eyes blinking totally out of control and no longer even in sync with one another.

"Good," Spike said huskily into his ear, gently biting its lobe. "Just one more thing," she added as she rose out of her seat and leaned over to whisper in his ear again. "No keisters," she said, and then disappeared into one of the big jet's first class lavatories.

Jacko waited, afraid to look around the cabin, fully expecting all eyes to be on him. His paranoia told him that every word was probably overheard by everyone, passengers and crew members alike. He stole a glance across the aisle and, sure enough, Mrs. Bean was glaring at him as if Spike's every word was carried over the plane's public address system, announcing the impending tryst to one and all. He shrunk down into his seat and closed his eyes, wishing he was invisible. Jacko counted off the seconds, letting more than two minutes elapse and finally rose up out of his seat, nodding to Mrs. Bean, a guilty-as-sin grin already on his face, and nonchalantly strolled toward the lavatory door, whistling as he went. He stopped at the door and tapped three times as lightly and quickly as he could. The door suddenly swung open and Spike's bare arm reached out, grabbed his tie, yanked him inside and slammed the door behind him.

"Now, where were we?" Spike whispered.

"My *zuppa*?"

"Yes, your zuppa," she said, reaching for his zipper. She squirmed onto the sink, wrapping her long legs around him and said, "Tell me all about it."

There followed several minutes of them knocking around in the tiny space, making just enough noise to attract the attention of the cabin attendant who happened to be passing by. She lingered outside the door a moment, listening.

"Heat the oil," Jacko grunted.

"Yes, heat the oil!"

"Add the leeks and garlic."

"Yesyesyesleeksgarlic! Yes!"

"Now I put the mussels in," he snarled.

"Oh God, yes! Put the mussels in!"

"Sauté everything . . ."

"Yes!"

"Put the andouille sausage in . . ."

"Yes, put it all in, damn it!"

"Spicy . . ."

"Yes! Hot and spicy!"

"Four minutes more . . ."

"Yes! More! Minutes! More!"
"Serve!"
"Yes! Yes! Serve it to me!"
"It's hot . . ."
"Oh!"
"Hot!"
"Yes! There! Hot!"

The stewardess had heard enough and was actually blushing as she started to make her way down the aisle. Mrs. Bean, who had watched the whole thing, reached out to stop her, and asked what was going on.

"Cooking class," she replied, and continued on her way down the aisle, still blushing.

* * *

Less than an hour later Spike and Jacko were silently staring at the luggage conveyor that was snaking its way around the baggage claim area. It was empty except for their own bags which were yet to be retrieved and were now making their fifteenth pass right in front of them. They each eyed the luggage again in silence. Spike wasn't sure what she was feeling. Disbelief, shock, anger, embarrassment, stupidity, guilt or maybe a combination of everything. Or maybe, simply the beginnings of love. She turned to face Jacko, who had his hands thrust deep into his pockets and was staring at the ground in front of him. A sadder look on his face wasn't possible.

"You're not," she said, maybe for the fourth or fifth time.

"No. I'm not," he answered. Again.

"You're sure."

"Positive."

"I see."

"Sorry."

"No, don't be," she said.

"But I am."

"Don't be. I'm not."

"You're not?"

"No, I'm not."

"You're sure?"

"Positive."

"Okay. But you're just saying that."

"No, really. I'm not sorry at all. Besides, it was my idea, remember?"

"How could I forget?" Jacko said, a sheepish smile forming.

Silence again. Both of them alone with their thoughts. She, biting softly on her bottom lip. He, shifting his weight back and forth from one leg to the other. Jacko broke the silence.

"You're not the first, you know."

"Oh, great. Just what I needed to hear," Spike said.

"I didn't mean *that*. You know, up there."

"Oh."

"I meant...."

"I know."

"I mean, people are always telling me that I..."

"I know. I know."

"I should have known you might think I was..."

"No. It's all my fault."

"No it's not."

They both watched again as their bags went by on the endless conveyor, neither of them quite sure where to go from there.

"So, was I the first?" Spike asked, a smile now forming on *her* lips.

"You mean..."

"Yes."

"Of course you were!"

"Good."

"Was I? *You're* first, I mean. You know, in a plane?"

"Of course you were!"

"Good."

"Yes. Good."

"No, *very* good!" he said, and they both burst out laughing, causing everyone in the nearly empty baggage claim area to smile at them.

"Are you hungry, Miss Mahoney?"

"I am famished, Mr. *Kosciusko*!" she answered, no longer shocked or the least bit upset like she was twenty minutes ago upon learning that *that* was his real name.

Jacko looked up at the overhead flight information screen and quickly found what he wanted. A Pacific Air shuttle was scheduled to depart for San Francisco at 7:25 P.M. He checked his watch which was still on east coast time, and it read 10:05.

"Think you can handle the best Italian food in all of North America?"

"I don't know," she answered, a big smile on her face. "Does it beat your zuppa?"

"It might. It's where I got the recipe. Let me have your claim check," he said as he grabbed her hand and pulled her with him toward a nearby porter. He gave the man a twenty-dollar bill along with their claim checks and, pointing to their luggage on the conveyor platform, asked him to hold it somewhere safe for a few of hours. He took her hand again and they ran across the terminal to the Pacific Air counter where he bought two tickets to San Francisco. They raced as fast as their feet would carry them to the departure gate and boarded the plane with five minutes to spare. After a short flight and a cab ride that was almost as short they were in Napa Valley, seated in Jacko's favorite west coast restaurant, the appropriately named *La Vallata*. It was owned and operated by Valdo and Enzo Altadonna, two transplanted brothers from Hoboken, where they and Jacko had grown up. Valdo, who was in charge of the front room, made the fuss he always did as soon as Jacko entered, only more so seeing the beauty who was with him this night. Enzo, the chef, came out of the kitchen as soon as they were seated to personally welcome them and, upon hearing that they had just met, promised them a feast to remember the night with. Jacko was never offered a menu at La Vallata nor did he ever ask for one, preferring to put himself in Enzo's capable care. This night would be no different and, as always, Enzo did not disappoint. Course after course of what Spike called *a naughty orgy for her taste buds*, came parading to the table from the kitchen, along with the best wines the valley had to offer. They were there late into the evening, with both brothers eventually joining them for espressos, desserts and several rounds of after-dinner drinks. Valdo told them that they had just sold the restaurant and announced, to everyone's delight, that they were returning back east to open another one at the Jersey shore, on the popular resort Island known as the Reach.

Jacko and Spike promised to visit their new restaurant every chance they got. The brothers, totally ignoring the fact that the couple didn't even know each other a few hours ago, did their best to persuade them to get a place of their own on the Island. A good time was had by all, especially Spike who, at different times and with complete sincerity, whispered privately into each brother's ear that she intended to name her first-born after him, bringing a beaming smile first to the face of Valdo and, some minutes later, to that of Enzo. Amazingly, she would keep both promises and do just that in the years to come. Sort of.

When they were about ready to leave, Spike, with a lascivious look on her face and with her hand hidden under the table squeezing Jacko's thigh, told them she never had so fabulous a meal and, though she couldn't believe she ate all that she did, was craving some zuppa di pesce! Enzo was about to jump up and head for the kitchen but Jacko stopped him saying she was only joking. He shot Spike a scolding look that said *Bad girl*! Spike apologized, explaining it was a private joke and, kissing them both on the cheek, assured them she couldn't eat another thing. The Altadonna brothers cast a curious smile toward Jacko and, seeing them to the door, bade them a good night.

Six days later, as the trade show in Las Vegas was closing down, Spike and Jacko were married in one of the little chapels on the strip. The chapels would set a record for spur-of-the-moment weddings that day. Couples finding themselves in Las Vegas and in love on *seven-seven-seventy-seven* discovered that combination to be too powerful to ignore and with a spontaneity and gameness appropriate to the locale, kept every Justice of the Peace in town busy all day long and into the night.

A few years later Spike and Jacko Kosciusko *did* buy a brand new summer house on the Reach and frequented the Altadonnas' new establishment almost on a weekly basis. The restaurant, *La Sabbia,* Italian for *sand* was located on its own little sandy beach right on the bay and so was, again, very aptly named. More often than not Jacko and Spike were joined by some of their new friends and neighbors who, with one exception, shared their passion for world class food and wine. That exception being the neighbors to their immediate north, the Meshitskys who, at least for the first few years, managed to insinuate themselves into the lives and activities of the others, including evenings out.

J'net

Fun lovin' is what you'd call the people on Bay Vista, most of em. They all had kids so there was always a lot of activity what with the beach bein' just down the street and every family havin' a boat to enjoy water sports right out on the bay. Those Kosciuskos were maybe the zaniest of the lot. Really had me goin' the first time I met em, him tellin' me he was some sort of Martian from some crazy planet. Him and his wife always doin' somethin' nutty as all get out. Nutty nicknames too, Spike and Jacko. Speakin' of names, they had themselves a pair of twins right after they moved in and they went and named em Enzo and Valdo, of all things! Now he's Polish mind you and she's about as Irish as they come and they go and pick the most unusual Italian names possible for their two blond-as-could-be, blue-eyed little baby boys. Go figure. I once asked her about it but all she'd do was wink at me. Nutty. Named his boat "Just Visiting" to prove he was from another planet he'd always say. His brother's name was George but for some reason everybody called him Hymie. That's nutty too if you ask me. He and his brother would go fishin' just about every Saturday mornin' and every Saturday afternoon they'd come back at the cocktail hour and Spike and her sister-in-law Flo would have martinis all ready and waitin' for em right there on the dock. Jacko'd be bringin' the boat in toward the dock and he'd start announcin' the day's catch. Like he'd holler "Six nice blues" and Spike would echo it back and then he'd holler "Four good stripers" and she'd echo that too and if they got any crabs he'd holler "Twelve keepers" and she'd repeat that right back and so on until they came to the end of the ritual which never varied: He'd be gettin' close to the dock and he'd finally yell "No keisters!" and this time everybody on the whole bayfront would join in the echoin' includin' me and even Joe on several occasions and dependin' on the wind a resoundin' "No keisters" could sometimes be heard blocks away. I once asked her about how that got started too and once again all I got was a wink. So that sort of thing was typical of life on Bay Vista and if it wasn't the Kosciuskos providin' the fun then it was one of the other families who'd step in and pick up the slack. All in all there was never a dull moment and there was lots of entertainin' always goin at one or another's house mainly havin' to do with food and Joe and I were invited to many a dinner party over the years. Especially to the DiMarco house as they knew I was more than a little fond of Italian cooking, and Marco and Mona could cook Italian with the best of em. Course, Marco never stopped kiddin' me about my pronouncin' it the way I did but I couldn't help it. "Eye-talian" was just the way everybody said it growin' up down in Louisiana. Course, I'd tell him I was married to two "Eye-talians" and it never bothered either of em one bit. And he'd usually say somethin' a little on the risqué order in answer to that. He was always flirtin' with me and tryin' to embarrass me but I don't embarrass too easy so it never worked. I'd just tell him that I was more than twice his age with more than twice the experience and I would be happy to teach him a thing or two anytime Mona would let me and Mona would always say be my guest and he'd be the one who'd end up bein' embarrassed most of the time. Course Joe would also get a little embarrassed bein' that he was a bit of a party pooper when it came to speakin' pleasantries such as that. But it was all in good fun and we'd always leave the parties thinkin' nice thoughts about most of our neighbors. That's "Most" with a capital M.

Five
Killa da Bastaches Widda Kyness

Marco DiMarco was present at his wife Mona's birth. The circumstances that caused him to be there would make it difficult, if not entirely impossible, for anyone to construct a family tree that looked even remotely normal, especially after their daughter Mia was born. That's because Mia, while being Mona's daughter, technically speaking was also her second cousin. And, while Mia was Marco's daughter too, she was also his first cousin twice removed. The reason for this strange happenstance was that Mona's mother Josephine was Marco's first cousin, her being the daughter of Marco's mother's older sister who was also named Josephine. This first Josephine would actually be both a great aunt and a great-grandmother to Mia, while her younger sister Eleanor, being the second Josephine's aunt, would be Mona's great aunt and Mia's great-great-aunt and her grandmother too. And, as weird as it may sound little Mia would be, undeniably, *her own* second cousin once removed!

So it was that Marco, at age six in 1952 and too young to be allowed past the lobby, found himself waiting on the steps of Jacoby Hospital in the Bronx, eating a five-cent bag of potato chips purchased for him by his mother from Rueben's deli across the street just before she went in and up to the maternity ward where her niece was in labor with *his* second cousin once removed who, in turn, would give birth to their only daughter some twenty-six years later.

It wasn't until the potato chips were half gone that Marco peered into the bag, which in those days was made of a yellowish waxy type of paper and screen-printed in one color with the brand's logo and product information, that he noticed ants crawling all over the chips inside. Shuddering with disgust, he threw the bag into the gutter and spent the remainder of his waiting time sitting on the curb and spitting in non-stop mode until his mother finally came out to take him home. That incident was enough to forever leave him with a deep-seated dread of any and all insects. His revulsion to anything crawling was such that, in later years, he'd just point at a creepy offender and Mona would have to squish the life out of it for him. He'd tell her that was the least she could do since this minor phobia of his could probably be traced directly to the occasion of her birth and therefore she should take a responsible role in alleviating his qualm. Fortunately for him she had no problem whatsoever with that arrangement and the only times he reluctantly had to kill a bug himself were those times when he was alone and had no other choice.

Ironically, bugs, all manner of them, were a key factor in actually putting Marco in business in the early seventies and also resulted in his nearly going out of business soon thereafter. He had been working as a creative director at one of New York's leading ad agencies when a friend, who was an account executive at a rival shop, told him that a certain insecticide account would soon be up for grabs. A relatively small company with a small budget, the account in question felt their business wasn't getting the attention it deserved from the very large agency that currently handled their business and was quietly looking around for a new relationship. His friend went on to explain that he knew the top management at this company and offered to introduce Marco to them as a possible answer to their search, adding that it could be an opportunity for him to open his own shop with a nice little piece of business already on the books. Marco agreed, thinking why not give it a try.

After meeting with the company exccutives Marco was invited to make a presentation outlining his creative approach to market the company's insecticides. He was awarded the account based on his recommendation of using microscopic video photography that would depict insects at their hideous worst and over-filling the TV screen with frightful close-up images and dreadful accompanying sound effects that he promised would send horrified consumers rushing to stores in search of their products. Unfortunately he did too damn good a job and the truly atrocious and unimaginably loathsome, larger-than-life hairy monstrosities that he paraded across and, all too often, practically *through* viewers' TV screens were scaring the living bejeesus out of some people, himself included. Within a year he had the feeling his days were numbered with his one and only account. The success of the ad campaign could not be disputed. Sales had grown exponentially since the commercials started running but so had complaints from irate mothers whose kids were having nightmares. Marco read some of the consumer hate mail and didn't doubt for a second that they were sincere. The uglier-than-hell bugs were giving *him* nightmares too, in more ways than one. Even one consumer complaint was often reason enough to be fired in this business no matter how much the cash register was ringing. He'd heard rumors that the end to this particular agency/client relationship was already a fait accompli. He decided to call Pat Casey, the friend who had originally put him together with the client, figuring that if anyone knew the real scuttlebutt it would be him. They made a date to meet for a drink at P.J.

Clark's, Madison Avenue's most venerable haunt, that evening after work.

Marco was at the bar nursing his second scotch as Pat walked over and, slapping him on the back, said "Cheer up pal, nothing's forever right?"

"So it's true?"

"Got it right from the horse's mouth not more than an hour ago. I'm afraid you're history in the bug murdering business."

"That means I'm history in business *period*."

"Maybe not," Pat said, ordering a beer from the bartender. "I've got a friend who needs some help and I think the two of you would hit it off."

"What business is he in?"

"Not business. Politics."

"A political campaign? I've never done one."

"Doesn't mean you can't."

* * *

It was an off year for politics in that there was no national race being fought and, in New York, no major state-wide contests either, except for that of Attorney General. That office had been vacant since the previous A.G. suffered a stroke some months back and, while there were a few congressional seats up for grabs, the State Attorney General's race would make the most noise and be the most hotly contended battle of the season. It was a high-visibility office that often led to much bigger things. A shot at Mayor, Governor or U.S. Senator was in the cards for an aggressive A.G. who was ready to move up and the major party candidates were expected to hold nothing back in their respective campaigns to win the job. Joseph Conwell, the Democrat, and Dick Beeson, the Republican, were already almost household names, especially in the New York metropolitan area. Conwell was an overly verbose, four-term State Senator from Brooklyn and Beeson had been the most vocal City Councilman in New York in the last decade. Both camps had plenty of money and experienced campaign managers with solid organizations behind them. It was no secret that the two candidates didn't like each other and, though the race wasn't even in full swing yet, it was already showing signs of being as dirty as it gets.

It was a little-known fact, especially among the general public, that there was another declared candidate in the running. That was because he was all but invisible in the total scheme of things as the race was beginning to heat up. The major party candidates, their spokespersons, the media as well as all the political pundits barely acknowledged his existence, the early consensus being that he didn't have a snowball's chance in hell of even being a factor in the outcome. It was this Independent candidate, of course, who Pat Casey wanted to hook up with Marco, hoping that what was sorely lacking in campaign money-muscle might be compensated for with novel creativity, something that was never in short supply with Marco.

Dominic DeGange was a total unknown in political circles. He had no organization to speak of, it being comprised mainly of old classmates from his days at Fordham Law School whose only credentials were that they shared his idealism. Not too impressive or even appropriate considering this was a high-stakes political campaign that they somehow managed to talk him into. His campaign funds were laughable compared to the war chests that had been amassed by the other candidates. At first, this whole folly had been against his better judgment and now he couldn't believe he let it go on as long as it had. If truth be told, his personal politics suggested he shouldn't be trying to get *into* politics in the first place. Dominic DeGange just wasn't the kind of a guy that gets involved in the inherent ugliness and partisan propagandizing that seems to be the heart and soul of politics today. As Assistant District Attorney, he happened to be a pretty good criminal prosecutor when he believed the defendant to be guilty, but less than formidable if he had even the slightest doubt. And, conversely, most people, himself included, knew he would make a damn lousy defense lawyer, incapable of providing an advocacy of any real substance for practically *anyone* who he felt might be guilty of practically *anything*. So, a politician was the last thing Dominic wanted to be. But Attorney General, that was a different story. A loftier perch from which to go after the bad guys without having to answer to anyone. An important political post yes, but one in which he didn't have to be a politician. That was the only reason he reluctantly decided to give it a try when his friends first suggested it. But it was clear, if only to himself, that he didn't really stand a chance and now was probably the time to just quietly disappear from the whole affair. As if anyone would even notice his exit.

So, when Pat Casey called and suggested that he meet with Marco his first inclination was to decline. But he finally agreed to it for two reasons: As a favor to his longtime friend and because he had nothing to lose. And Marco agreed to the meeting for two reasons too: As a favor to a longtime friend and because he desperately needed some new business.

* * *

Pino's, a tiny restaurant on Arthur Avenue in the Bronx, was a favorite of Marco's and he'd suggested they meet there. It wasn't exactly the best place to hold an important meeting, and definitely not if you needed any kind of privacy. But the food couldn't be beat anywhere in the city and the prices were such that, regardless of how things went and who picked up the check, it wouldn't be too painful on the wallet.

As usual, the place was mobbed when Marco, after being caught in terrible traffic, arrived almost thirty minutes late. He tried scanning the room, jumping in place to peer over a sea of humanity that was happily crammed like sardines into the bar area, sipping drinks and patiently waiting for a table. He finally spotted someone that looked like the person whose picture he had from a local newspaper article on all the candidates who were running in the upcoming elections. He managed to squeeze through the throng to the man standing near the bar and, apologizing for being late, introduced himself. Dominic looked relieved that he wasn't being stood up and confessed he probably would have left had it not been for the incredible aromas wafting from the nearby tables. It was true, as everyone seemed mesmerized in anticipation of the wonderful food to come.

"Wait until you taste it. You won't believe it," Marco assured him. He waved to Giancarlo behind the bar, who waved back and yelled over the din in a heavy Italian accent that it would about fifteen minutes for a table. Dominic, pleased at that news, especially since he'd deduced during his wait that *Pino's* didn't take reservations, suggested they order drinks which they did, Jack Daniels for himself and Chivas for Marco. What Dominic *didn't* know was that Giancarlo's "fifteen minutes" could actually *mean* fifteen minutes or it could just as easily mean two hours and Marco thought it better to keep that to himself for the moment. That's the way it was at *Pino's* and no one ever complained. The food was that good. Fortunately it wouldn't be too long a wait that night. Two more rounds and forty minutes later they were seated facing each other at the middle of a long table, shoulder to shoulder with total strangers on either side of them. That's also the way it was at *Pino's*. You were served "family style" which at *Pino's* meant big platters of outrageously good food in such quantities that it was customary to offer some to people sitting next to you, and they would do the same. The informality was such that it wasn't uncommon at all for someone you'd met not fifteen minutes earlier to be reaching over with a piece of crusty bread to sop up some of the wondrous sauce from whatever dish you happened to be eating at the time.

Pino's had been attracting people from virtually every social and economic stratum imaginable for decades. They would come from all parts of the city and suburbs beyond. On any given night the person sitting on one side of you might be dressed to the nines in formal or near-formal evening wear while a person on the other side would be in jeans and a tee-shirt, which both Marco and Dominic noticed was the case this night.

Pino's had no menu. The kitchen prepared several appetizers, pastas, fish and sea food, veal, beef, chicken and vegetable platters every night. Waiters tried as best they could to limit people's choices based on what parties next to them were having, this in an effort to encourage conviviality among its patrons. And it always seemed to work as conversation and food sampling were the norm in the loud and bustling room. It hardly mattered what dishes were set before you because everything they served was simply the best food you ever tasted.

The bar area being too crowded and noisy to even think, Marco and Dominic had thus far limited their conversation to small talk. Once seated and more relaxed they began to loosen up, no doubt helped by three drinks each and a surprisingly good house Chianti they were now drinking. Dominic, whose natural inhibitions would ordinarily have prevented him from speaking candidly with all those people within earshot, was uncharacteristically open and forthcoming and Marco, fast warming to this new acquaintance, was likewise exhibiting an expansive temperament. Their easy-going naturalness with each other and others around them only increased as food began to arrive.

Digging into an extraordinary hot antipasto, Dominic held nothing back in relating his dire campaign predicament to Marco and Marco held nothing back in commiserating with him on the sorry situation. Neither did the well-dressed woman sitting to the right of Dominic who had been hanging on his every word. Emphatically *tsk-tsking* and shaking her head in sympathetic agreement, she was now spooning some of her scungilli onto both of their plates, dismissing with a wave of her hand Dominic's polite but totally insincere attempt to decline it. Dominic thanked her and reciprocated by sending two giant shrimp oreganata and some stuffed mushrooms her way, and continued grumbling about the shameful state of political affairs that seemed stacked against decent, honest people who were trying to enter the field.

The focus of the conversation was now on the two major candidates, with Dominic contending that both men were hard-boiled products of the corrupt, old-line party machines that ruled everything that happened in city, county and state government in New York. Someone at the table behind Marco chimed in, saying "*Anybody in office as long as those two have to be crooks!*" This was met with a "*Here! Here!*" from two people across the room. By the time a monstrous platter of mussels marinara arrived and was set briefly in front of Marco and Dominic before traveling east to the nice scungilli-lady and her husband and then west to a friendly young couple dressed in very comfy-looking grubs, whose own platters, one piled almost a foot high with fried calamari and the other with clams swimming in white wine and garlic, made their respective stops in the opposite directions, Mr. Conwell and Mr. Beeson were loudly being referred to as those "*greedy no-good thieving bastards*" by all six new-found friends as well as several others at nearby tables. And by the time the pasta and meat courses came, accompanied by another bottle of Chianti, both candidates had been downgraded again, this time to those "*filthy sons of bitches who should rot in hell!*" and that proclamation was being vociferously passed with concurrent sounds of clinking glasses echoing throughout the restaurant.

Marco, caught up in the euphoria of the moment, not to mention the euphoria of the wine, stood up and declared the upcoming campaign "*a crusade pitting good against evil,*" receiving unanimous applause from everyone including the restaurant staff who was now urging him on. And on he went, outlining to one and all, the master plan which he was hatching at breakneck speed as he spoke that he promised would surely "*expose the bastards for what they were!*" Marco continued almost nonstop, pausing only occasionally to down another shot of Anisette which he'd pour from the bottle left on the table to accompany espressos. By the time he had finished there wasn't a soul in the room who didn't believe that Dominic was the only honest politician left on the face of the earth as well as the best attorney who ever lived. The oratory received a standing ovation, the crowded room now convinced they were in the presence of a master strategist, a genius who would make Dominic DeGange the next Attorney General of the great State of New York. The look on Dominic's face told Marco that he believed it too.

*   *   *

Marco woke the next morning not sure if he was still

alive. He slowly opened one bleary eye to see what time it was but the alarm clock wasn't there. He rolled over to look on the other nightstand but that side of the room was spinning like a gyro. He turned back the other way and the room was still again. He did it again. Spinning. Then back again. Still. Spinning, still, spinning, still. His head was pounding with the same unbearable ferocity whichever way he faced. His neck was stiff as a board. His mouth felt like he'd tried eating a tennis ball. He rubbed at his eyes and was surprised to find no blood on his fingertips. Eyes that hurt the way his did *should* be bleeding. He was sure that his stomach was filled with snakes. Big ones. This was no ordinary hangover. This one was hell-bent on sadistic punishment and would not be denied. He didn't dare try getting up knowing his head would explode if he did.

He lay there trying to remember the night before, but could only piece together fragments. He remembered the food. That he couldn't forget. And Dominic of course. And that, as usual, Pat had been right because they really *did* hit it off pretty good. He could picture some of the people there. He remembered being exhilarated but not the reason why. He finally fell back into a fitful sleep punctuated by images of his giant insects, sitting with him at a table in Pino's drinking Anisette through straws and eating his missing alarm clock. He woke about an hour later to an incessantly ringing phone.

Dominic let the phone ring twelve times before giving up. Had he let it ring just once more Marco would been able to reach it in time. He'd rolled out of bed hitting the floor with a heavy thud and, thinking it best to keep his center of gravity as low as possible, crawled across the room to where the phone was but it stopped ringing just as he was about to pick it up. He sat there on the floor, his back against the wall, cradling the phone in his lap for five minutes and tried to rejoin the living. It was only then that he realized his pillow was stuck to the side of his face. *Dried dribble,* he said to himself, then added *I hope!* He attempted to get up and was surprised to be able to stand on his own two feet holding on to nothing but the phone which he still clutched tightly in both hands. He was feeling enormously proud of himself when the phone rang again, making him jump at the sudden noise.

Dominic, thinking he may have dialed the wrong number, decided to try again. This time Marco answered on the second ring in a painfully hoarse voice that Dominic thought sounded strangely demonic. So did Marco, evidently, because he tried it again.

"Hello," he said in a voice that even he didn't believe was his.

"Marco?" came a cautious reply from Dominic.

"Afraid so."

"Good morning! It's Dominic DeGange."

"Then how could it be *good?*"

"Ah, I see. I guess your head feels as bad as mine."

"Worse, I can assure you."

"Well, I just wanted to thank you for a fabulous dinner."

"Did I pick up the tab?" Marco asked.

"Of course you did. I'm the client. That's the way it works."

"Does that mean you hired me?"

"How could I *not* hire you after last night? I just want to make sure you know how impressed I was with your strategy for the campaign. And not just me," he added. "Everyone there felt the same way! They all told me that."

"I see," Marco said, unable to remember a fucking word he uttered the night before. "What part of the strategy did you like the best?" he asked, trying to draw Dominic out.

"Why, the '*Big Idea*' of course!" he lied. The truth was

that he couldn't remember anything Marco said either and that phrase was the only thing that had stuck in his brain.

"Right, the *big idea*. Anything in particular about it that really turned you on?" he asked, trying to pry something, *anything,* out of him once more.

"No, I liked the whole *big idea* in its entirety, actually," Dominic said. "Listen, Marco . . . we don't have a minute to spare. I want you to get started right away. Let's meet tomorrow. I'm anxious to hear you elaborate further on your plan. We can go over budgets and anything else you think is necessary at that time too, okay?"

"Sure, tomorrow," Marco said, and they made arrangements to meet at Dominic's apartment in Greenwich Village. They hung up and Marco rested his aching head in the palms of his hands and thought to himself, *Shit, now what?*

* * *

Later that afternoon Marco hailed a cab and told the driver to take him to Arthur Avenue in the Bronx. He got there about three o'clock and stepped inside Pino's which, except for the table of employees at the back, was eerily empty. Giancarlo was eating along with eight others, his waiters and kitchen staff, before beginning their final preparation for that evening's rush. As soon as they saw him the entire table erupted with applause and cheers of "*bravo*" and "*professore.*" Giancarlo pulled an empty chair up next to his and motioned for Marco to come join them. As soon as he was seated a plate appeared in front of him and before he knew it he was helping himself to things that he was sure he'd never had before. He may not have known exactly what he was eating, but he knew was it was outrageously good. Most of the conversation was in Italian and Marco was able to grasp very little of it, having been raised in a household where English had already become the dominant language.

When there was a lull in the conversation, Marco explained why he was back so soon and they all laughed, refusing in good fun to immediately tell him what his *big idea* of the previous night was. When Giancarlo thought they'd had enough fun at his expense he put his arm around Marco's shoulder and solemnly said, "My frein', you big idea isa you gonna killa da bastaches widda kyness!"

Marco looked at him, then looked around the table at the others who were all smiling, then back to Giancarlo again and said very slowly, as if he was afraid to speak the words, "I'm going to kill the bastards with kindness?"

"Thassa right, my frein', thassa you big idea," and the others all nodded in agreement.

"You mean *that's it?* That's *all* of it?" Marco asked incredulously. "That's what everyone made all the fuss about?" They all nodded in unison again except, this time, they weren't smiling any longer.

Giancarlo, finally seeing the point, put his arm around Marco once more as if to console him and offered, "It sounda betta lass night," and, again, nods from the others. Marco lowered his head into the palms of his hands for the second time that day and said, "*Shit, now what?*"

* * *

Marco had recovered from his hangover of the previous day by the time he left for his scheduled meeting with Dominic. But he didn't feel any better. The fact of the matter was that, for the first time in his career, he was bankrupt in the idea department. The more he tried to figure out what "*kill the bastards with kindness*" was supposed to mean, the more hare-brained it sounded. Yet there must be something to it he kept telling himself on the cab ride downtown. Why else would everybody be so enamored with it? Especially Dominic. He had the feeling that there might be a germ of an idea there, but he just couldn't put his finger on it. On the other hand, there was always the slim chance that Giancarlo and the others were mistaken about what he said, English not being their strongest asset. He was hoping against hope that that was the case, and intended to try to draw some details out of Dominic once more before making a total ass of himself.

Dominic greeted him and, ushering him in, said that he'd taken the liberty of inviting three of his closest friends, the ones responsible for his being in the race, to join them, explaining they all planned to play an active role in the campaign.

That's just fucking dandy! Marco said to himself, thinking that was the last thing he needed right now.

They made their way into the living room and Dominic introduced him first to a polite, good-looking young man who was a lawyer in the employ of the city named Devon Grief, then to a scrawny, bearded little guy who had beady little eyes hiding behind thick, rimless glasses named Sebastian Fish. Marco instantly decided he didn't like him.

"It's about time you got here," Marco heard a curiously familiar voice say behind him and turned to see a young woman backing through a swinging door leading from the kitchen carrying a tray loaded with sodas, beer and assorted snacks. As she turned, Marco was stunned, putting it mildly, to see the smiling face of his cousin Mona who, after setting the tray down, walked over and grabbed him by both shoulders and kissed him, a little too long it seemed, squarely on the mouth.

"Small world, huh?" she said, stepping back and putting her hands on her hips, striking a coquettish pose as, still shocked, he took her in. It was a hot day in the middle of June. She was barefoot and wore a halter top and faded, frayed jeans cut so short that both the front and back pockets stuck out well below the bottoms onto two long, perfect legs. *Damn fetching,* Marco thought, then silently scolded himself with, "*She's your cousin, for Chrissake!*"

He hadn't seen his cousin, actually his "*first cousin once removed*" in almost two years. He remembered hearing that she had recently graduated from Fordham Law School. As he would learn in the next few minutes that's where Mona, and Devon, who was also a student there, met Dominic. He was a few years older and teaching a course there and the three of them had become friends. Sebastian owned a nearby café that they spent a lot of time in and had somehow managed to get himself included in their wild campaign idea. Marco looked around the room and wondered what the people heading up the other campaigns would think if they could see the little group assembled here. He doubted they'd be shaking in their boots.

"Well, Marco," Dominic finally said. "When Mona heard who was going to be in charge of things here she said, '*If Marco DiMarco can't get you elected nobody can.*' So I guess I made the right choice!"

Sebastian looked anxious to hear what Marco had to say and, judging from his demeanor, seemed predisposed to not liking whatever it was. Devon had rolled up his sleeves and looked all business. Dominic looked nervous as hell, as if he had no inkling of what was coming. Mona sat beaming at him from the sofa, her legs crossed, one bare foot swinging ever so slightly. Marco was transfixed on her legs and, realizing it, silently scolded himself again, "*Stop it dammit!*"

"So, Dominic tells us you've solved the whole problem," Sebastian said.

"Oh, I don't know, what do *you* think about it?" Marco

replied, trying to get Sebastian to give him some sort of hint as to what he'd already heard.

"Dominic wouldn't tell us anything about anything until you got here," Devon said. "Come on, don't keep us in suspense any longer!"

"I see," Marco answered, deciding to try one last desperate ploy. "Dominic here is our candidate, right? I think it only appropriate that he let you in on it."

"No, no! I won't hear of any such thing!" Dominic almost shouted in panic and, catching himself, continued more calmly. "You gave birth to the concept. The *big idea* is yours. It should come from your lips and yours alone! I insist on it!"

All eyes were now on Marco and they weren't about to wander elsewhere until they heard what he had to say. Marco stood up and, trying to buy some time, began pacing the length of the room back and forth in front of them, stroking his chin and feigning a deep concentration on things of great importance. What he really was thinking was this: *What the fuck am I doing here!?!*

"Gentlemen . . . and *lady*," he quickly added, his eyes lingering again on Mona's legs. "What I propose to do is this . . ." Marco turned away from them, afraid to see their reactions, cleared his throat and blurted out, "Kill the bastards with kindness!"

He waited for them to say something. Curse him. Stone him. Do anything that would just let him out of this ridiculous mess but there was only silence. He slowly turned around and looked at each of them one by one. Sebastian seemed smugly pleased. Devon, who sat poised with a yellow legal pad and pen in his hands, looked perplexed, like he had missed something important and was now trying to hide it. Dominic looked to be completely paralyzed. Mona, beaming as big a beam as anyone ever beamed before, looked from one to the other of her friends and said, "See? I *told* you he was a genius!"

* * *

The crush that Mona had on Marco throughout their childhood was always thought of as cute by the entire family and everyone constantly kidded Marco about it. A family gathering or holiday didn't go by without him hearing, more than once, *"Careful Marco, she's gonna vamp you someday!"* Mona's open adoration for her older cousin continued into young adulthood when Marco started making what, at least to everyone in their close-knit family, was considered *big money* in his first few jobs in advertising. She thought it was really cool that he wore thirty-dollar shirts when ones costing six or seven bucks were more than adequate for everyone else in her world.

So Marco wasn't really surprised that Mona jumped up from the sofa during that first meeting of the campaign's brain trust and launched into a passionate dissertation on what she viewed as the most brilliant idea she had ever heard and a strategy that would render their opponents all but impotent in their ability to fight back. What *did* surprise Marco was that she did a fairly reasonable job at articulating many of the things that he himself wasn't able to during his cab ride earlier. He had been thinking or, more accurately, *hoping* there was some substance to whatever he was espousing in the restaurant the other night but, before Mona started to put some meat on the bones of the so-called idea, he just wasn't convinced. So Marco sat down and let Mona knock herself out ranting about how the public was fed up with all the negative aspects of political advertising that was always being shoved down their throats and that here was a chance to really take the high road and separate Dominic from the crowd and make him stand out as the truly great and decent person that he was while having exactly the opposite effect on Conwell and Beeson in the eyes of the voters and so on and so forth, etc., etc., until everyone in the room, even weasely, smarmy Sebastian, agreed that Marco may indeed be a genius.

The discussion moved on to other issues like who would do what, and eventually to campaign finances which immediately put a damper on everyone's enthusiasm, especially Marco's. It was estimated that they had about two-percent of what the other candidates were thought to have and that realization cast a definite air of gloom and doom on the proceedings. Everyone seemed to slump back into their seats dejectedly and waited for Marco to say what they all thought was surely the inevitable. Something to the effect of *"Oh well, it was great fun while it lasted."* But instead, they watched as Marco again started pacing back and forth the length of the room, though this time truly deep in thought. At least five minutes went by without anyone saying a word. Marco finally stopped and popped a can of beer and took a long swallow.

"That just means we have to make our money work a hundred times harder than theirs" he said reassuringly and resumed his pacing.

"How do we do that?" Dominic asked.

"Leave that to me," he answered, still pacing but now with a knowing smile on his face.

"What is it? Tell us!" Devon pleaded.

"Not just yet," Marco said, preferring not to reveal the executional gem that was forming in his head before he had time to flush it out.

"Just leave it to me," he repeated, looking over at Mona on the sofa, her long legs now crossed Indian style, a beer in one hand and a big, salty pretzel in the other, once again beaming at him.

* * *

What transpired over the next twelve weeks leading up to the election was absolutely great for the DeGange campaign. Marco could not have orchestrated it better even if he tried. As predicted, the race for Attorney General was getting all the attention in the media and campaign spending by the two major candidates was exceeding earlier expectations. Also as predicted, it was turning out to be the ugliest campaign New York had ever seen. Conwell and Beeson were spewing venom to such a degree that the sheer depths that they were sinking to became the real story. They were laying into one another with a ferocity that was almost unbelievable to the general public and, although the mudslinging was all anyone, especially the press, was talking about, both camps were unable to change the course they had embarked on. The attacks were now becoming more personal in nature and recently even the candidates' immediate families had begun trading insults with each other. And it didn't seem to matter that the public had long ago been turned off by the pure distastefulness of the whole effort. It was as if the two campaigns were halfway through the final, steepest slope of a raging rollercoaster ride and the downward momentum was so great that changing direction was all but impossible. This filthiest of all campaigns would only end when both camps had run out of money or when Election Day had finally arrived. Marco, knowing that both of these ends were just around the corner, was delighted with the prospect.

It was now just ten days to the election and the DeGange campaign had yet to run a single ad. They had picked up about a dozen more volunteers and a little more money along the way and by now everyone was growing impatient with Marco's seeming inactivity, even Dominic. "*Antsy*" was the word Sebastian would use as often as he could, somehow knowing that it sent shivers down Marco's spine every time he heard it. But Marco stood firm and, with Mona's unswerving loyalty and help, managed to convince them that he knew what he was doing, even though he himself was a tiny bit afraid that what he planned was quite possibly too little and too late. But, given what little he had to work with, he really didn't have much choice and was convinced it was their only chance. The serious lack of funds in the coffer necessitated his waiting until the very last minute before spending it.

He had busied himself over the past weeks making sure his plan was fine-tuned, all the while keeping it a total secret from everyone but Mona and, to a lesser degree, Dominic, both of whose invaluable help was needed if he was to pull it off. Not only would his media spending be at anemic levels, he had to keep production costs to a bare minimum as well, all in an effort to get every last mile out of every available dollar he had.

The time had finally arrived to begin setting things in motion. A flurry of small "*teaser*" ads started to appear in all of the local newspapers and on transit posters throughout the state's major metropolitan centers. This was supplemented with five-second radio spots that, in order to keep costs down, used Mona's voice. They all delivered essentially the same message:

JUST WHEN YOU THOUGHT YOU HAD ENOUGH OF NEGATIVE POLITICAL ADVERTISING, ALONG COMES DOMINIC DeGANGE!!!

And

**NEGATIVE POLITICAL ADVERTISING
WILL BE TAKEN TO A NEW
PLATEAU BY DOMINIC DeGANGE!!!**

And

**ATTENTION MR. CONWELL AND MR. BEESON . . .
YOU'RE ABOUT TO BE TAUGHT A LESSON IN
NEGATIVE ADVERTISING BY YOUR
RIVAL, MR. DOMINIC DeGANGE!!!**

Marco spent almost half of his entire budget on these teasers which literally blanketed the major cities all across the state for six straight days. Almost no one had even heard of Dominic before and now they couldn't wait to find out who he was and what he was all about. Marco's tiny three-room office above a liquor store on Third Avenue in Manhattan had served as Campaign Headquarters and it was now being inundated with calls from all the news media as well as a few lame attempts from poorly disguised members of the opposition camps. Everyone was clamoring to find out what was going on. The volunteers were under strict orders not to reveal a thing, although they couldn't even if they wanted to.

Amazingly, Marco had succeeded in keeping his "*piece de resistance*" a total secret from everyone except Mona and, until very recently, even Dominic himself. The mystery continued for two more days when small space ads appeared on page three in every major newspaper in the state. The premium he paid for this guaranteed positioning was one of only two extravagances Marco allowed himself. The ads were designed to look like news stories and carried the headline "*Dominic DeGange To Air Negative TV Ad Tonight*" followed by two paragraphs of copy in which it informed readers when and where to tune in to see the commercial. Local news outlets picked up on the ploy, further spreading the word about what was fast turning into a media event. Marco had negotiated with a major network for one ninety-second spot to run as a "*roadblock*" in every locale in the entire state at precisely 9 P.M. that night. This was to be the second extravagance he paid a premium for and one that he gambled would return the big results that were needed. It was a gamble that paid off in spades as, for the first time in history, people actually switched channels *en mass* that evening for the sole purpose of watching a commercial! And a *political* one at that!

What they saw and heard was this: Screens went briefly black and then white type scrolled across with a voice-over by Mona reading, *"The following is a negative ad for Dominic DeGange, the Independent Candidate for Attorney General of the State of New York."* That was followed by seventy seconds of Dominic, who fortunately had an engaging speaking voice, facing into the camera and delivering his message in a serious, straightforward manner. What was unusual, though, was that Marco had shot the spot in color, had it converted to black and white and then aired it almost entirely, at least for the first thirty seconds or so, in negative form. The compelling visual effect kept viewers' eyes glued to the set and cleverly paid off on all the advance hype and promise of it being a *negative* commercial. The humor of it wasn't lost on anyone and it resulted in the TV audience being immediately receptive to Dominic and his message. Not to mention that it very effectively reinforced the mountain of bad feelings that had already built up in the public mindset about the dirty campaign the other candidates had engaged in for what seemed had been an eternity.

Viewers watched as Dominic's image slowly and ever so imperceptibly morphed from negative black and white into rich full color, revealing a surprisingly handsome face to go along with a nice voice that was now speaking uncommonly kind words about his opponents. Dominic told his audience that Joseph Conwell and Dick Beeson were both undoubtedly outstanding individuals and superb public servants who he was sure would make great leaders and promised to support either of them should they ever decide to run for important offices such as mayor or governor. He went on to say that the office of Attorney General didn't need a good politician, which his opponents unquestionably were. What it needed was a good prosecutor, which they weren't. But of course that's exactly what he was. He said that Conwell and Beeson deserved to get their votes, but for a job that they'd really be good at, probably in the not-to-distant future. Right now, though, it was important to make sure we get a real prosecutor for Attorney General!

The entire viewing audience, including Conwell and Beeson and their cohorts, were left with one unmistakable, irrefutable thought: Regardless of the kind words this refreshingly likable candidate had uttered about them, Conwell and Beeson were the bastards and Dominic was the good guy. And to make sure that point was driven home Marco closed the spot by freezing the smiling face of Dominic with a legend across the bottom of the screen that read: **DeGange . . . DeGood Guy!** The screen slowly went to black again, the words, in vivid yellow, moving up to the middle and reinforced by Mona, her voice speaking them for all to hear.

The commercial aired only that once but had the clout of some of the most expensive advertising ever to run in so focused a market. It became the talk of all the media reports the following day and even made some of the national newscasts. It received so much publicity just prior to Election Day, being shown in its entirety over and over again countless times on a variety of news and talk shows that the PR value alone was worth every cent the other candidates had spent throughout the campaign combined. The Conwell and Beeson camps scrambled to defuse the excitement it was causing but were out of time and could do nothing about the sudden hemorrhaging of their fast-sinking campaigns or the seeming juggernaut that Dominic had gained literally overnight on the impending election.

Dominic was elected in such a landslide that news stories later questioned whether anyone other than friends and family voted for poor Conwell and Beeson, both of whom were never heard from again in New York politics.

Regarding Marco and Mona, one thing led to another during the time they spent working together on the campaign and, shortly after it ended, decided to legitimize what some members of their family called their shameful *living in sin*. They were married, with Dominic as the best man, and had a big party at *Pino's*. Like the Kosciuskos, a few years later they too bought a summer house on the Reach, residing next door to a four-hundred-plus-pound conniving lowlife named Lloyd Meshitsky.

J'net

Kids is what I enjoyed most about life on Bay Vista. Every family there had em and they never failed to make you feel lucky to be alive and luckier still to be able to summer on the Reach every year. I watched em grow and start maturin' for twelve years straight. There was somethin' about the Island that seemed to contribute to kids bein' nicer than other kids in general. At least that's the way I viewed it. Every one of them kids was just as polite as could be whenever they were around me and Joe. Well, almost every one of em. Let's see, there was eighteen of em in all. The DiMarcos only had one, a beautiful little girl. Then there was those cute blue-eyed, blond-haired Kosciusko twins with their Eye-talian names. The Gorshins had three, the oldest a boy, and two darlin' little girls. The Drakes had four in all, two boys and two girls, all of em real friendly. The Mullin and Elias families each had two teenage sons and the Pearlsteins had one little girl and one baby boy. Course, then we had those two Meshitsky kids. Now here's the strangest thing. Mia DiMarco, Clarissa Pearlstein and Amy Gorshin were all born on the same exact day. So that first summer, when the kids' fifth birthday, September 2nd, was gettin' close it was decided that a big party was in order. And that's how the annual block party first got started. Every year thereafter on the Sunday before Labor Day we'd all gather down on the stones between the Kosciusko house and the Gorshin house at about five o'clock and that's when the festivities would start. Everybody spent the whole day cookin' up their best specialties and the wine would start flowin' and the music started and the kids would jump in the bay and several of the grownups would usually do the same thing before the night was over, only, what with the amount of libations bein' consumed, they'd never bother to put a bathing suit on, just jump right in with their clothes on. Me and Joe would marvel at the whole thing, like watchin' a bunch of kids that never grew up. But it was always the best time everyone had all summer and though it meant the end of the season we'd all be lookin' forward to it just the same. Even Joe would loosen up some and act a little like a kid himself on occasion. Speakin' of kids, bringin' em into the world is what Doctor Gorshin and Doctor Drake were busy doin' all week long back home. Among other things I suppose. Ob-Gyn was their specialty and I understand they had the busiest practice of its kind in all of Philadelphia. I don't know if that's the kind of thing that gets into the Guinness record book but if it did those two would surely be in the runnin' for some kinda recognition and that's a fact. Why, I once heard they'd birth eighty babies a month on average between just the two of em plus even more on weekends by another doctor that works with em. That sure qualifies as an over-abundance of baby-deliverin' no matter how you look at it if you ask me. I guess you'd say they were good at what they did. Lord knows they were in need of some serious R&R by the end of the week. And they were pretty good at that too. The R&R I mean. Rich Drake was what you'd call a serious fisherman. He'd sometimes be miles and miles out to sea for days at a time. His boat was good for that kinda sport fishin'. That was his therapy I suppose. Max Gorshin would rather stick around and do some serious partyin'. You'd always know when Max was seriously partyin' cause that's when you'd hear him start singin' Dean Martin songs. "That's Amore" was clearly among his favorites, I can attest to that. He'd belt it out no matter where he happened to be. Whether he'd be relaxin' with a cigar up on his deck or sometimes after a few too many after-dinner Sambucas at that favorite Eye-talian restaurant of theirs. Anyway, as I was sayin' it was the kids that I loved watchin' have such a great time. And it was the kids who would always reflect the kind of families they were from. You could tell a lot about the parents just by watchin' the kids. At least I always could. And the more I watched the more I learned. I don't remember exactly when I started to pay a lot of attention to the Meshitsky boy. Maybe after that incident with Joe and his father when we were in the yard. But I did watch him a good deal. Course, he never noticed it. I was just an old lady of no real import to him. But he should have noticed me, cause then he would have realized I was on to him about a host of things he thought no one would ever get wind of. I kinda felt like I was a detective workin' undercover. This was not a good kid. I started savin' up some of the things I learned about him. Kept most of it to myself. Except for his damn cacklin'. AAHK AAHK AAHK. No one ever knew it was him makin' all them seagull sounds until I told em. He'd hide out of sight when he started up and I guess if I wasn't spyin' on him so much I may not have known it was him either. I must admit though, as annoyin' as it was, he got pretty good at it after a while. But it always irked me no end when I heard him cause he'd never let up. So one day I just told everybody it was him. Didn't faze him in the least though. He just started doin' it out in the open after that, and even though everybody on the block would tell him enough was enough, he still kept it up. I'd sometimes tell Joe about other things I saw him do or about somethin' that looked suspicious to me. I guess I was the first one to know for sure that Seth Meshitsky was evil. Except for his own family. Course, they never did anything about anything anyway when it came to controlin' his conduct. Just looked the other way and let him run wild. Eventually everyone on Bay Vista came to that realization but it took some longer than others. About his bein' evil I mean. After a few years everybody started to notice things but usually only after he'd do something really harmful. Me, I noticed more than others did cause I was watchin' him. But most times he got away with his damnable behavior. He was a sneaky, hateful child who showed no goodness toward anyone and managed to get worse as he grew up. I guess some people are just plain rotten to the core. That's "Rotten" with a capital R.

Six
Zag on This!

Max Gorshin, Rich Drake and Michael "*Swifty*" Pearlstein grew up together in Philadelphia and remained best friends their whole lives. They did pretty much everything together. They went to the same schools, started playing golf together every chance they could, triple-dated, hung out, studied and caroused with one another all the way through their college years. Their constant companionship was interrupted only briefly when they went to different graduate schools and resumed again immediately thereafter. It was generally understood that Max and Rich would become doctors. It was likewise always assumed that Michael, because of his quick wit, fast thinking and a natural gift of gab would go on to become a lawyer, which he did, acquiring his nickname early on along the way. Max and Rich chose the same field of medicine to specialize in and, soon after completing their internships, became partners and opened their first Ob-Gyn office together.

A day didn't go by, especially early in their careers, that Swifty wasn't bemoaning the fact that, while he was spending his days mired in mountains of research and legal documents, his buddies were spending *their* days with naked women. And a day didn't pass that he didn't let them know it. The doctors, of course, never missed an opportunity to rub it in either. Especially on days when they were scheduled to do something together after work and Swifty would meet them at their office. They would make him sit in the waiting room eying the last patients of the day as they left, knowing that the more attractive the woman the worse it was for Swifty, who would drive himself nuts with jealousy, conjuring up images of the various women back in the examination rooms with one or the other of his friends.

Dinner conversations on those evenings, or any evenings for that matter, were usually variations on the same theme.

"What, I don't look like I could be a doctor?" Swifty would plead his case.

"Hmm. Not really," Rich might answer.

"So I'll wear a white coat."

"No. Not a good idea," Max, enjoying it immensely, would chime in.

"Okay, how about this. I'll just be a breast checker. Maybe just one day a week. There's no harm in that. Waddya say?"

"What's a breast checker?"

"You know. Examining breasts. I could do that."

"That wouldn't be an examination, Swifty. It would be fondling."

"That's what *you* two do."

"It's different. We're *licensed* to fondle. You're not."

"Fuck you. Fondle *this*," Swifty would say, grabbing his crotch.

Max and Rich would erupt in laughter.

"You're both licensed lechers."

"No, you have to be a certain age to be lecherous. We're not there yet. We'll apply for our lechers' licenses in twenty or thirty years," Rich said.

"Yeah," Max chimed in. "Right now we're content with just our *lucky licenses*."

"Fuck you."

"It's your own fault," Rich said. "You could've gone to med school with us."

"Yeah, that's right," Max agreed. "You zigged when you should've zagged."

"Fuck you. Zag on *this!*"

And that's the way it would go, not really changing much even after they were all married, continuing right on into middle age or, as Swifty would call it, *lecher* age.

Rich would be the first of the three to marry and, like the good Irish Catholics that he and his wife Irene were, wasted no time at all in growing a family. They had two boys and two girls in such quick succession that Swifty offered to let Rich have his nickname, adding that his partner Max couldn't deliver babies as fast as he was making them.

Max was next to get married, to a former girlfriend of Swifty's named Carrie and Swifty then married Carrie's best friend Daphne, and both couples were soon starting families of their own.

Rich was already familiar with the Reach, having vacationed there many times with his family while growing up. An avid boater and fisherman, he began to look for a summer home there as soon as their practice started to flourish. And, to describe the Gorshin-Drake practice as flourishing was an understatement. In fact, they had so many patients and were delivering so many babies at one point that the Philadelphia medical community was enviously referring to their office as the *Baby Boom*. Swifty's law practice was also doing pretty well by then though, as he always complained, sans the naked women.

All three families decided to take a day trip to the shore one Saturday to check out what Rich had been raving about and see what he was planning to buy. As it turned out, not only Rich, but Max and Swifty as well all ended up buying summer homes on the Reach. The Drakes and the Gorshins on the water and the Pearlsteins right across the street in a tiny enclave called Bay Vista. They all resided in close proximity to the Kosciuskos and the DiMarcos. Unfortunately, they were also in close proximity to the person Swifty would later dub the *Thieving, Over-Stuffed Human Kielbasa.*

J'net

Seems people are always confidin' in me. I don't know why but they do. Especially the women though sometimes men will do it too. Joe Jr. does all the time. Probably I'm the mother he never knew havin' lost her so early. But mostly it's the women. I guess I'm a good listener. That and maybe cause I'm the sort they feel won't betray their confidences. Which I don't, except in rare instances. Funny how Joe Jr. is so different from his father. A real talker. At least to me he is. Course, he'd never be able to talk to his father about some of the things he does with me. He really opens up at times. Like tellin' me how it was with him and his friend Kev when they were young and discoverin' together about their queerness and all. Funny how birds of a feather always seem to find each other. Part of nature I suppose. Anyway, it was durin' one of those talks that Joe Jr. told me somethin' I suspected for some time, namely that the Meshitsky boy was a queer too. Course, I pretty much had that figured out already from all my observations of him through the years. But he confirmed it for me. Wouldn't go into details but said he found out when he was up for Joe's funeral. Had somethin' to do with Father Kev and that's about as far as he'd go. None of my business anyway and no skin off my back, that's for sure. Just one more thing I got to learn about some of the people on Bay Vista. Seems a good deal of the things I learned about people on Bay Vista, at least all the unpleasant things, all had somethin' or other to do with the Meshitsky family. Course, most often it was Lloyd that was the culprit but his son Seth contributed a fair share to the malfeasance too. The apple doesn't fall far from the tree as the sayin' goes and Seth had about as big a louse for a father as ever there lived. He was settin' bad examples for him from the day he was born. And, bein' evil to begin with, emulatin' his father sorta came natural for him. Anyway, I did learn about a good deal of the wrongdoin' perpetrated by Lloyd but probably not nearly all of it. And I learned about most of it from the women on the block usually long after the deed was done. Course, they all swore me to secrecy bein' they, or more accurately their husbands, were sort of ashamed at havin' been taken advantage of. Funny about men. Even though they themselves are the victims for some strange reason they'd rather keep tight-lipped about it. Women are different though. They're the talkers and they're the ones confided in me. Seems Lloyd didn't discriminate much at all among his neighbors on the Reach when it came time to inflictin' his particular brand of nefariousness. At one time or another over the years he managed to enrich himself with ill-gotten gains from each one of em and was yet to suffer any consequences for it. So there I was bein' the recipient of all this secret information from the women of Bay Vista who, mind you, never once spoke even a word of it to each other but somehow thought it was okay to let me in on. That's what I mean when I say people just naturally confided in me. Course, I learned about other instances of Lloyd's thievin' ways too, mostly involvin' regular workin' people not gettin' paid after doin' one thing or another for him, usually small maintenance type jobs now and then. Joe always said those are the ones he ought to be fearful of but nobody ever did much except file somethin' called a mechanic's lien on his house, whatever that is. All I know for sure is nobody ever recouped a single nickel of what Lloyd stole from em. At least not until the very end. That's "End" with a capital E.

Seven
Woodies Would Happen

Kevin Flaherty and Joe Cooper Jr. became friends when they were in the sixth grade. They attended the area's only public elementary school and, later, the high school, both of which were located on the mainland. Kevin, along with his family, were all devout Catholics and would have much preferred his attending Saint Josephat's on the Reach but that school's tuition was beyond their limited means. Kevin and his family had to be satisfied with his just being a church altar boy there. By the time they reached high school Kevin and Joe were practically inseparable. Individually, they often grappled with the steadily growing realization that they were different from their other friends and classmates but were privately both happy and thankful for the camaraderie that had developed between the two of them. They were basically good kids and well liked by everyone, even some of the girls who would occasionally show more than a passing interest but were never successful in generating a reciprocal response. Attempts at flirtation slid off the boys' backs like water off of ducks and, inexplicably, rather than being nonplussed or feeling rejection, most girls were generally content with just being good friends.

    Becoming a good swimmer usually went hand in hand with growing up on the Reach and that was certainly true for young Kevin and Joe. They both joined their high school's swimming team in their sophomore year. Having no pool of its own, the school had a long-standing arrangement with Saint Josephat's to use its extensive and modern indoor facilities for the team's practice sessions twice each week. And that's where the boys were no longer able to avoid the inevitable.

The testosterone that begins to rage in teenage boys at pubescence will always make itself apparent regardless of the appropriateness of the moment. Just the slightest glimpse of lacy underwear or a fleeting peek at any and all cleavage is more than enough to produce an immediate, universally identical and totally uncontrollable result in most adolescent males the world over. And the looser the trousers the more visible its manifestation. Indeed, if you were to throw two naked, normal, red-blooded teenage boys into an open locker-room shower facility with a bunch of naked teenage girls, the results would be hard, no pun intended, to hide. Now, put two naked, *not-so-normal,* red-blooded teenage boys into that same shower with a bunch of other naked *boys* and guess what would happen? Woodies would happen. Woodies hard enough to hit a baseball out of the park with.

Kevin and Joe were lucky. Miraculously, they managed to grab for their towels in time to conceal what was happening before anyone had noticed and, in perfect, though somewhat exaggerated lockstep, quickly made their way into the locker room where, in a matter of minutes and without so much as a word to each other, they were back in their street clothes and gone with no one the wiser. They both quit the swim team the very next day.

At times the boys each harbored suspicions, not to mention *hope,* about the other but, up to that point, had never once broached the subject. Neither of them was quite ready to admit, even to themselves, what deep down they were coming to know was the truth. The incident in the shower was a defining moment in their lives and in their friendship, each boy feeling as if the weight of the world was suddenly lifted from his shoulders, so glad were they to be able to confront together what, until that day, had always been a dreaded reality. What followed could be considered a *coming out* party of sorts, albeit a secret one to everyone but themselves. It would be some years before people knew with any certainty that they were gay. Their remaining high school years were spent in a *discovery* mode and, while there were occasions when they did indulge in certain things with each other, those instances were very few and neither thought of them, even remotely, as real romance. Rather, they each viewed them merely as a confirmation of a newly comprehended fact and an appreciation of their uniquely galvanized friendship.

At sixteen, Kevin had taken a summer job with one of the Island's best caterers. Almost every weekend was spent working private parties in homes of some of the Reach's most affluent summer visitors. One such person was Glen Pedersen, a hugely successful fashion photographer from New York who owned a palatial ocean-front home in Dune City where he hosted lavish, day-long parties every week. The home was one of the more magnificent ones on the Reach and Kevin worked alternately as a server, bartender, pool boy, cook, cleaner-upper and whatever else was necessary, seeing to the every need of some of New York's most *beautiful* people during these opulent, twelve-hour fun fests.

The house, a ten bedroom mansion really, had every amenity imaginable both inside and out, including its main attraction: a custom-designed, multi-level video room with six giant rear-screen projection systems. The room was decorated entirely in endless shades of red on red. Carpet, acoustical ceiling, flocked wall paper, light sconces complete with low-wattage red bulbs and the furniture itself, all red. Entering it for the first time was like walking into a French whore's boudoir, except there was no bed. Instead, the room was filled with fifteen identical, made-to-order, overly soft, red leather reclining love seats equipped with drink holders, ashtrays, a smoker compartment stocked with the best marijuana and hashish that money could buy and a whisper-quiet, heated, multi-targeted internal massage mechanism. The love seats were scattered about the room, seemingly at random but, upon closer examination, one would realize that each was quite strategically placed at different angles and at different elevations, providing its occupants with a modicum of privacy while also affording them an unobstructed view of at least three of the six movie screens.

This was the room that the last of the late-night revelers would drift to as the party wound down and on any given Saturday evening up to thirty guests might be found there until the wee hours of the morning.

Glen Pedersen was as flamboyant a homosexual as ever existed, and his party guests were generally gay, lesbian or, at minimum, bisexual. And they were very active and indiscriminant in their carnal pursuits. That was partly the reason that one of Glen's houseboy's nighttime duties was to keep each of the six giant screens filled with different non-stop images of the best and most current decadence and perversion the pornographic industry had to offer. And it was *only* the images, the sound having been muted on all of the VCR players in favor of a special instrumental-only compilation of show tunes that played on a continuous loop during the entire night's screenings. Quite the unique audio-visual combo . . . hard-body butt-shtupping to the musical accompaniment of "*My Boy Bill*" from *Carousel*.

Kevin's duties for his catering employer customarily included returning to the Pedersen home the next morning and help with the clean-up chores. The video tapes were always rented from the Island's porn shop in South Beach by the houseboy prior to each party. Glen, who had taken an immediate liking to young Kevin, would usually ask him to return them the next day, thereby saving his houseboy the twelve-mile trip each way to the southern end of the Island. Kevin was only too happy to comply with the request as it afforded him the opportunity to watch most of them with Joe before they were due back. And, the crisp hundred dollar bill that Glen gave him each week for his troubles certainly did nothing to dampen his enthusiasm to be of service.

Kevin never stopped raving about the Pedersen house and Joe, curious to see it for himself, accompanied him one day on his morning-after task. There was no disputing the grandeur of the place and Joe could do nothing but marvel at it. He was much less impressed though, with its owner. In fact, as he would later tell Kevin, a little *repelled* was the way he described feeling upon meeting him.

"I don't know, Kev, there's something creepy about him."

"That's just your first impression. He's really a nice guy."

"I shook his hand, Kev. It felt *smarmy*."

"What's that? Like sweaty?"

"No, it's different. It's worse."

"Worse how?"

"Like the way you feel when you see *Liberace*. Sends shivers down your spine."

"Speak for yourself. I like Liberace. So do millions of other people. *Straight* people too, for your information."

"Yeah, right. Go figure."

"You should give him the benefit of the doubt, Joe. He grows on you."

"Yeah, I'll bet."

And it was true, at least in Kevin's case. It wasn't long before Glen became completely smitten with him and not too long after that when he began sharing his love seat with him in the screening room. On the days after those occasions Kevin received an additional five hundred dollars over and above the usual C-note he got for returning the tapes. And it progressed from there. There were a few instances when they'd retire to the bedroom where one or more of Glen's friends would also participate. Kevin's bonus after those events was an amazing one thousand dollars. Kevin was absolutely giddy over Glen's generosity and couldn't keep it a secret from his best friend even if he wanted to, although that thought never even crossed his mind. He didn't expect Joe's reaction to be what it was and it stunned him. Joe was just plain shocked, and could do nothing other than stare at him for several moments in utter disbelief before he was able to speak.

"Kev, you're *prostituting* yourself?!?"

"They're *gifts*, Joe."

"Bullshit!"

Kevin fell silent, avoiding eye contact.

"I don't fucking *believe* this, Kev."

"Divinity School costs money, Joe," he finally answered weakly, still unable to look his friend squarely in the face.

"*Jesusfuckingchrist!*"

"Joe, stop."

"Jesusfuckingchrist!" he said again, adding "You're being a *whore*, Kev!"

"Joe, please don't say that."

"Well, it's *true!*"

"I meant 'Jesus with the F word' . . . please don't say that."

Joe just shook his head, saying, this time to himself, *Jesusfuckingchrist!* Not another word was ever spoken on the subject by either of them. Their friendship was shaken a tiny bit on that day but it would survive.

J'net

Me and Joe decided to celebrate our seventh weddin' anniversary where we met, down in Belize. We spent almost two weeks roamin' all over the country seein' just about everything there was to be seen, then we spent two days at that jungle lodge where we first laid eyes on each other. Course, the evenin' scotches we sipped up on the rooftop terrace those two nights seemed to be a bit more pleasurable than usual. Better even than you can imagine. And I swear if them howler monkeys weren't serenadin' especially for us somewhere out there in the pitch black then I don't know what all. Joe thought so too, I could tell. We spent a few more days just relaxin' at our little hut, and then headed up to Belize City to have lunch with Joe Jr. before we had to leave for the States again. Seems Joe Jr. never stopped advancin' at the bank he worked at. Assistant vice president was the title he had at the time. Course, he was real modest sayin' that it wasn't a big deal and that there was a whole slew of others with the same title. Didn't stop Joe from bein' as proud as could be though, that's for sure. We were sittin' at a little table at an outdoor café just diagonally across the street from the bank and we were havin' a grand time gettin' caught up on all the goin's-on over the last two years that we didn't see each other. Course, Joe Jr. took pains not to dwell on personal stuff, especially on anything havin' to do with the "other" Joe in his life. He was still feelin' uncomfortable on that score even though I always assured him as best I could in my letters that his father was pretty much acceptin' of the situation. Anyway, there we were havin' a good ol' time when out of the blue Joe drops his spoon into his bowl of conch soup splashin' everything in sight includin' his brand new seersucker jacket and I see his eyes narrow into these little slits and his face sorta drains of its usual handsome *ruddy color. Me and Joe Jr. both followed his gaze to see what was upsettin' him so much and as soon as we did the gasp I made was so loud it shocked me almost as much as what my eyes were takin' in. Right there in front of the bank, not fifty feet away, was the fattest man to ever hail a cab on the streets of Belize City carryin' with one index finger a big black duffel bag that judgin' by the way it was swayin' in the breeze was nothin' if not absolutely empty. An old two-toned Pontiac with the word "taxi" crudely hand painted on its sides pulled up to the curb and we watched as it groaned audibly and listed heavily to one side under the weight of its new passenger who had struggled mightily to squeeze into the back seat. The cab slowly started movin' down the street and we all stared after it dumbfounded as it crawled along makin' sparks every few feet with its right rear bumper scrapin' against the pavement. It turned the corner and when it was out of sight we all just looked at one another and believe you me no words could've said any clearer what our expressions did, namely "what in hell and damnation is Lloyd Meshitsky doin down here?" Joe Jr. only saw Lloyd once on one of his trips to the Reach so I was sorta surprised that he even recognized him but he's sharp as a tack in that regard and I guess I shouldn't put somethin' like that past him. Anyway, after we got over the near stroke we practically had seein' what we did Joe Jr. excused himself sayin' he'd be back in a few minutes and scooted across the plaza to see what he could learn about it. He was back pretty fast and told us that sure enough Lloyd had just opened an account at the bank but the bankin' laws bein' what they were down there, namely bein' centered around secrecy, there wasn't much else he could tell us. He went on to explain that the main reason for the Belize economy bein' what it is and why it's becomin' so popular is the fact so much off-shore money is gettin' poured into it. Most of what he was sayin' was goin' right over my head especially all that business about off-shore trusts and asset protection and tax-free tradin' and privacy this and privacy that and IBCs whatever that is. About all I could understand was that it was all based on keepin' ev-*

erything secret. A lot like in Switzerland apparently, he told us, where there usually ain't even a person's name on most accounts, just a number havin' five digits. Needless to say seein' him there sure worked on us in the curiosity department from that moment on. Well, I was to learn that wasn't the last trip Lloyd made to Belize. Seems he went down two or three times a year never stayin' more than a day at a time so nobody ever missed him, not that any of us had the least bit of interest in his comin's and goin's in the first place. I learned this from Shirley who was no different from the other women on Bay Vista when it came to confidin' in me. But that's where the similarities stopped. I really enjoyed the other girls but Shirley was a little hard to take and usually I didn't have much choice havin' been caught off guard and not bein' able to extricate myself without seemin' to be rude. But it was real tedious conversin' with Shirley, most of what she had to say bein' sorta inane and not the kind of subjects that would hold your interest. Plus she let it be known that she leaned toward havin' certain racist tendencies, always usin' the word "nigger" like it was okay. And for her I guess it was, havin' heard it used so many times by Lloyd. Never once really exhibitin' that she had a mind of her own I guess she'd been followin' Lloyd's lead since the day she met him. Course, it was a fact that the Reach was one of the whitest places on earth with the percentage of people of color of any kind probably bein' minuscule compared to most other areas of the country. But just seein' a person anywhere on the Island whose dark complexion might not be purely the result of the sun was enough to set Shirley off to tellin' anybody who'd listen that she spotted a "nigger" that day. Like it was the kinda news that should start people worryin'. Truth of the matter was that it was stuff like that that made most people think of her and her family as what's known as "white trash" and that was the real worrisome thing if you ask me. And there were other things she'd say that really got my craw up. Like she pitied some people she knew, mostly old friends and even some relatives who didn't have the things that she did. Like her five carat diamond ring in particular. Said she was embarrassed for them. So much so that she would sometimes turn the ring around on her finger and close her hand into a fist so the "poor people" wouldn't have to be envious of her. Demonstrated it for me too, like I should be proud of her. Course, it wasn't even a real diamond. Neither were the stones in her bracelet, a "tennis bracelet" I think she called it. Same with her earrings too. Somethin' known as Cubic Zirconias is what they really were. Course, her skunk husband never bothered to tell her that and she didn't find out they were practically worthless till many years later when she tried to sell em. But that's a whole other story. Anyway, seein' Lloyd down in Belize and hearin' about his other trips from Shirley was the way I found out that he was most likely stashin' a lot of money outside the country. And that's when I really started smellin' a rat. That's "Rat" with a capital R.

Eight
Like a Supine Whirling Dervish

Lloyd Meshitsky majored in accounting at Stockton State College, graduating in 1965. He was able to gain an entry-level position at one of the "*big seven*" accounting firms in Manhattan where he spent six very unspectacular years crunching numbers in a department of the company known as "*the pits.*" That was what everyone called the second floor of the corporate headquarters building where the Proving Unit, the department's real name, was located. It was referred to by its nickname partly because the second floor was the lowest floor of the skyscraper building that actually functioned as office space, the ground floor being a sprawling chrome and glass lobby housing a coffee shop, newsstand, a bootblack and a few retail shops. The main reason though was because working in that department *was* the pits. Its sole function, and that of all its personnel, was to verify the accuracy of the firm's more senior accountants. The department, hardly a hotbed of motivation, seemed to operate in an exaggerated state of numbness that was all its own. Considering the absence of anything even remotely approaching excitement that all but permeated the monolithic firm, or the whole profession for that matter, the Proving Unit indeed proved every day to live up to its slangy moniker and well-earned reputation.

Lloyd had taken the CPA exam twice during this period

and had flunked each time. That, he told himself, was the reason he failed to advance in the firm. A bigger reason, and one that he would never even consider, was that no one liked him. He was a dullard stuck in a dull job and a pathological liar. He was a moocher of anything and everything he could get away with. Half empty cans of soda. Subway tokens. Food. *Especially* food. He would borrow money, a dollar here, five dollars there, at least once from every co-worker in his department without once ever paying it back. Nor did he ever intend to. He was loud, had an abrasive personality and he was physically repulsive to anyone he came in contact with. At age twenty-eight, and standing six-feet-three-inches tall, he was already morbidly obese, carrying a load of three-hundred-forty pounds along with a repugnant, sour pungency unique to overly fat people everywhere.

So, it was no surprise that when Lloyd took and failed the CPA exam a third time, he did what would have been unthinkable for most people but totally in character for him. He bought a bottle of the cheapest domestic champagne his local liquor store had and, with all the bravado he could muster, showed up at work and loudly announced that he had finally triumphed over those who had conspired to hold him back and, further irritating everyone as only he could, advised his co-workers and supervisors alike that he henceforth wished to be addressed as "*Lloyd Meshitsky, CPA.*" Inexplicably, no one ever thought to question this display of braggadocio, and as soon as a position opened up elsewhere in the firm his immediate supervisor as well as the department manager vigorously recommended him for the promotion, so eager were they to finally be rid of him. For Lloyd, the fact that he could get away with so brazen an act of deceit only served to embolden him to go on to bigger and better things in the future.

* * *

The move to the firm's Professional Practices Unit came with a two thousand dollar raise and Lloyd couldn't be happier in his new job situation. The PPU had a client base primarily composed of people in the medical and legal professions and Lloyd's job was spent in the field, making monthly visits to a list of doctors' offices to update their books and perform routine accounting services. He lived alone in a one-bedroom hovel in a run-down section of Newark and so was delighted that his territory was northern New Jersey. He was delighted too that his job came with an expense account that he was soon padding to the tune of fifty to sixty dollars a week without drawing any suspicion at all from his employers. This was money he put to the best use possible as far as he was concerned: his usual Friday-night excursion to a seedy bar and grill in the Tunnely section of New Jersey for beer and an all-you-can-eat roast beef buffet that left him with plenty of cash to spare for the services of one of the sallow hookers that were always loitering in the vicinity.

Lloyd was treated with a perfunctory politeness by his clients and their office staff which, in his egocentric mind, he erroneously interpreted as a new-found respect, attributable to his bogus status of CPA. And he never missed an opportunity to reinforce the sham, making sure that *that* professional designation was verbalized to every new acquaintance he made. It became such a permanent appendage to his name that, after a while, he actually started to believe it himself. Lloyd's ostentatious manner knew no bounds, often insisting to prove his prowess as the "*numbers man*" he claimed to be by forcing people to sit through a demonstration of a trick he once memorized from an activity book when he was just a kid. He called it his "*Incredible Calculating Conundrum*," always boasting that he, and only he, possessed the mathematical skill to have created it. Reactions would vary depending on the person on the receiving end of the riddle. Some would be mildly impressed and would want to know how it was done and these were the ones Lloyd liked because it made him feel superior and important. Others would be bored and not the least bit interested in pursuing the issue beyond the time they had already spent humoring him. These people Lloyd labeled as not being worthy of further efforts to enlighten and wrote them off as way too insignificant to bother with. This was Lloyd's *"Incredible Calculating Conundrum"*:

He'd start by writing the following five-digit number on a piece of paper, and asking the person to put it in his or her pocket:	**24262**
He would then write a four-digit number on another piece of paper (arriving at it by eliminating the first '**2**' from the previous sequence and adding it to the last '**2**' in that sequence making *that* number a '**4**') resulting in:	**4264**
He'd then ask the person for *any* four-digit number, for example:	**9137**
Lloyd would then put another four-digit sequence below *it*, secretly making sure that, when added to the sequence directly above, each of the four columns always adds up to '**9**':	**0862**
He would again ask the person for *any* four-digit number, for example:	**1391**
He'd supply four more numbers once again making sure that, when added to the four above them, each column would again add up to '**9**':	**8608**
He'd then ask the person to add all five sequences and it would always match what was in their pocket:	**24262**

It didn't matter to Lloyd that he never bothered to try to figure out how the numbers riddle actually worked. All that mattered was that he was able to impress some of the people from time to time. "*Lloyd's Conundrum*" was one of the first things people would be exposed to after meeting him. It became second nature for him to demonstrate it the first chance he got, and as natural a part of his manner as announcing his phony CPA status upon introducing himself to someone for the first time.

*   *   *

Lloyd had settled into a routine in his new job and soon found himself unable to control the envy building up inside him. In time, his every waking moment was filled with pure, green-eyed jealousy over knowing how much money his clients were making. He'd daydream while doing his bookkeeping work and often lay awake at night fantasizing about having as much money as even the least wealthy of his clients. His resentment grew to the point of his thinking of them as "*those doctors*," part of the great conspiracy against him that his paranoia had long ago conjured up. It never ceased to amaze him, though, that some of these same people with all their money actually looked to him, earning all of $18,500 a year, for financial advice.

After more than a year in his current form of job drudgery, Lloyd had become so discontent that he decided to test the waters with an idea that he'd been formulating. He selected one of his clients and confided in him that he was contemplating starting his own private CPA practice and wondered whether the doctor might consider allowing him to continue in that new capacity. He promised a more personal service than he was now able to provide given all the procedural constraints imposed on him by being part of such a large, inflexible organization and added he'd also be able to reduce his hourly rates substantially since he wouldn't have the costly overhead of his current employer. Getting more and better service at a lower cost was pretty hard to argue with so of course the doctor told Lloyd that he could count him in. So did almost all of the others and it wasn't long before Lloyd was making more than twice his old salary. Making more money and being his own boss agreed mightily with Lloyd and, as if the new-found euphoria he was savoring weren't enough, fate was about to deal him a hand that would forever change his life and plant him firmly on the road to a small fortune of ill-gained wealth.

Lloyd always enjoyed more than his fair share of good luck. Much, if not all, of every windfall he would eventually receive could be traced to one particular instance of his being in the right place at the right time. That instance being one of his monthly visits to the office of a client, Dr. Charles Wilner, an oncologist in Morris County, on the same day that Shirley Bershadski was there receiving some very bad news about her gravely ill father, Seth. Dr. Wilner was advising Shirley that her father's lung cancer had progressed to where it was now indeed terminal and that, given the severity of his condition, he felt it was time for her to begin putting his affairs in order. Sensing that Shirley hadn't the slightest idea where to begin, the doctor suggested that his accountant Lloyd, who happened to be right down the hall that day, might be a source of some good advice. He hurried off to find Lloyd, quickly explained the situation to him and asked if he wouldn't mind having a word with the poor girl, who was waiting to meet him in the doctor's private office. Lloyd, eager as always to see if there was anything to be gained for himself, promptly agreed and rushed right down to introduce himself.

Throwing open the door, Lloyd practically burst into the room startling Shirley out of the deep melancholy that had overcome her after the doctor left.

Ignoring the obvious sadness of her situation and flashing a big, toothy grin, he bellowed, "Lloyd Meshitsky, CPA" then, with all the sensitivity of a withered, sun-baked turd, added, "Here to save the day!"

"Shirley Bershadski. Pleased to meet you," Shirley replied weakly, reaching up to shake Lloyd's clammy, outstretched hand and feeling that the room was suddenly a lot smaller than it was moments ago.

Lloyd studied the blank look on her face and, his paranoia kicking in, was hoping he didn't already blow an opportunity. Shirley smiled then. At least Lloyd *thought* it was a smile although he wasn't positive. He should *know* when a female is smiling at him because it was so rare an occurrence, but Shirley's expression *also* looked as if she were about to cry. Her features were such that it was a toss-up. She had one of those really wide mouths with thick puffy lips that, at the moment, were pressed tightly together making her mouth seem even wider than it was. Fortunately, her whole head was a little on the wide side and she had a wide, flat nose to go along with all the other wideness so, all in all, things weren't totally out of sync. Lloyd noticed that she had a light growth of fine facial hair on her cheeks and upper lip that matched the blonde head of scraggly hair that hung down to her neck. She was extraordinarily big-boned with masculine muscle tonality and exaggerated, almost cartoonish-looking joints. Lloyd knew he'd seen people with these same characteristics before but he couldn't place exactly where or when. *Aboriginal Australian* could have been a fairly accurate description but he wasn't able to immediately make that association. But, a beauty, she wasn't. *That* was for certain.

Lloyd finally decided that Shirley *was* smiling, figuring

that if she were going to cry she would have started to by now. He also decided that, even with all of her physical imperfections, she was still a damn sight better than the street-walking skanks he was used to picking up in Tunnely every Friday night. And they *never* smiled at him.

"So, Doc says you have a problem that perhaps needs my help."

"Well, I'm not sure," she answered, losing the smile.

Lloyd tried to guess what she meant. Was it that she didn't really need help? Or was it that she didn't think he was the man that could help her? True to his paranoia, he opted for the latter and tried to think of something to say to impress her.

"I get sixty-five an hour," he lied, as he nonchalantly hoisted one huge haunch and, in the same motion, tried sitting on the arm of a nearby sofa, instantly breaking its leg and causing it to lurch forward, depositing him squarely on his fat ass with such a violent thud that it shook Dr. Wilner's wall of diplomas and plaques into comical disarray.

"Oh my God!" Shirley gasped, jumping out of her seat and retreating several steps away from the behemoth now sprawled on the floor before her. Lloyd struggled to his feet as fast as he could, entirely misreading her reaction. Believing that hearing his inflated fee was what shocked her, and not his mishap, he instantly switched gears and assumed an air of patronizing magnanimousness.

"But, for you dear lady, and given the dire set of circumstances you now find yourself in, I shall consider slashing my customary compensation."

Shirley just stood there, not sure what to say. Lloyd tried seizing the moment once again and, reaching out and proffering a totally spurious comforting hand toward her shoulder, guided her to a chair near the doctor's desk, saying "Sit here, dear lady. I'd like to show you something that I believe will ease your concerns." Taking a seat across from her, he explained that what she most needed at this difficult time was someone who understood *numbers* and could help her navigate the rough waters that lay ahead. Lloyd then launched into a demonstration of his conundrum. Well, never had anyone paid such close attention to his performance before. And never in all the years that he'd been doing it had anyone been so completely astounded with its outcome. Shirley made him do it again, of course changing the random sets of numbers she provided and her amazement at the end was no less animated than before. And the smile that was now most definitely stretched across her face buoyed Lloyd's egotistical self-esteem to a height never before experienced, causing him to make an offer that was, for him, about as uncharacteristic as one could be. Uncharacteristic because it was the first and last time he would ever even *think* of relinquishing a single, solitary dollar that he didn't have to.

"I shall waive my normal consultation fee in return for the pleasure of your company for dinner. How is Saturday?"

Shirley's smile was replaced with the perplexed look of someone who didn't know where she was nor how she got there. Lloyd took her silence to mean yes.

"Good. Let's say seven-thirty. At your place. We can discuss your unfortunate predicament at that time." Then, handing her a pen and a piece of note paper from the desk, he instructed her to write down her address which, as if hypnotized, she did and handed it back to him. Pocketing the slip of paper, as well as the expensive looking pen along with it, he took her hand in his and, mustering all the pretend-chivalry he could, bent low and loudly kissed it. Shirley could do nothing but stare at the now very moist back of her hand without uttering a sound.

Lloyd turned and walked toward the door, saying over

his shoulder as he did, "Meat and potatoes will do fine. And beer."

* * *

Muscatel is a sweet dessert wine made from the Muscat grape. After sherry and port it is probably the third most popular of all after-dinner wines. The grape is cultivated in many parts of the world, most notably Italy, France and California. The very good ones are usually called *Black Muscat* or, in the case of Italy, *Muscato,* and can be quite expensive. There are also a number of not so noteworthy standard versions that range from cheap to extremely cheap and it was these that enjoyed a period of high sales volume in the U.S. during the fifties and sixties, especially on college campuses.

That was a time before the term *date rape* even existed and certainly before drugs whose sole purpose is to facilitate that particular transgression were created. Today, though illegal, those drugs are readily available to anyone who really wants to obtain them. They have formal, chemical-based, medical-sounding names such as *Gamma Hydroxy Butrate (GHB)* and *Rohypnol* but are more commonly referred to by their slangy street names such as *"Easy Lay," "Liquid Dream"* or *"Get-Her-To-Bed."*

While the *term* "date rape" or its specially formulated expeditors might not have been in existence when Lloyd was in college, the act itself *was* and the popular means to that end for males having that proclivity was the very dependable, exceedingly affordable muscatel. Lloyd, who could be counted as being among this deplorable group, actually owed every sexual encounter he ever had, up to the time he began frequenting prostitutes, to that sweet, remarkably intoxicating libation.

So, it was no surprise then that when Lloyd knocked on

Shirley's door that Saturday evening he held under his arm not a box of candies, and not a bunch of flowers. No, what Lloyd held under his arm for his lady-fair that night was a bottle of really sweet, really cheap muscatel.

* * *

Shirley had stressed for days about what exactly to prepare for dinner and finally settled on things that were hard to ruin. Knowing he had requested meat and potatoes eased her anxiety somewhat and decided that London broil would be fairly easy. Take care that it doesn't get overcooked and slice it properly was all she really had to remember. She went shopping on Saturday morning and picked out the biggest one she could find in her supermarket's meat case. She opted for French fries over mashed potatoes and, remembering a time at an amusement park when she had them covered with gobs of melted cheese, thought *that* would be something he might really enjoy. She put a large squeeze container of Cheez Whiz into her cart along with a package of Pillsbury buttermilk biscuits. Then, knowing Lloyd was an extremely huge man, she grabbed a second package just to make sure. From the frozen food aisle she found a two-pound bag of French fried potatoes, crinkle-cut of course, the better to hold the cheese sauce. A can of Franco-American brown gravy for the meat and a package of frozen Brussels sprouts that just called for boiling would complete the dinner. A perfect meal, and a hearty one too she thought, to serve to such a large and important man. An accomplished, successful CPA. Remembering at the last minute that he had mentioned beer, she picked up two six-packs of Schlitz on the way home and began making the final preparations for the evening's big event.

If Shirley wasn't already nervous enough as she was

tending to the last-minute details of making sure everything was in order before Lloyd arrived, hearing him at the door a full half hour early raised her anxiety level several planes higher. She greeted Lloyd at the door and led him into the dining room where, without being asked, he took a seat, clearly conveying his readiness for food. Awkward and apologetic, Shirley told him she needed just a few more minutes and scurried off to get him a cold beer. Rushing back, she found him strumming his fingers and hulking over what, until that very moment, Shirley had always thought of as an impressively large table. She handed Lloyd a can of beer which he popped and, ignoring the glass she set on the table, downed without stopping for air. She quickly got him another and began skittering back and forth from the kitchen to the dining room readying the table for dinner while listening to Lloyd boast about how fortunate his doctor clients were to have him. He went on and on, taking great pains to make sure Shirley understood that his clients would be in terrible financial shape were it not for him and his ability to handle their affairs. About all that Shirley was able to understand for sure though, was that this was a subject that she *couldn't begin* to understand and probably never would. She found everything he was saying impossible to follow and was in awe of Lloyd's obvious extraordinary knowledge and acumen about all things involving money and finance. In point of fact though, Lloyd was spewing pure gibberish, having concluded fairly early-on that Shirley wasn't exactly the brightest bulb in the big chandelier. His only purpose in blabbering away was to continue to impress her and see where it would lead. A free dinner was already a certainty and, he thought, who knows what else might be in the offing.

Shirley realized a little too late that in her attempt to comprehend his ramblings she must have lost her concentration, which was not all that uncommon for her. She knew that London broil was supposed to be sliced on an angle but that wasn't what she did. Seeing the results of her knife-wielding didn't really surprise her either. Nor was she surprised that she overcooked it. She was used to doing things that she couldn't explain, in this case carving an entire five-pound piece of too-well-done meat without one slice having been cut as it should be, on a bias. Shirley did what she always did when things like this happened. She just sighed and frowned, never worrying too much about why they did, and proceeded to try hiding her error by covering the entire platter with gravy.

"Ah, what a beautiful sight," Lloyd said as she set the platter on the table. "What, pray tell, is it?"

"London broil," Shirley said, momentarily ashamed that even with all the gravy, her carving had made the dish unrecognizable.

"Mmm. And this?" he said, pointing to another huge platter piled high with lumpy, orange goop.

"French fries. With Cheez Whiz."

"And that?" pointing this time to a large bowl of yellowish, grayish, greenish things swimming in a murky liquid.

"They're Brussels sprouts," Shirley answered, adding, "They might need some salt."

"Exotic little minx, aren't you? *London, France, Brussels,*" Lloyd said, licking his chops and shoving the edge of a napkin into his collar. "I don't get to eat much foreign food. This is a real treat for me. Here, have some wine," he said, pouring the muscatel into her glass right up to the brim and popping another can of beer for himself.

Shirley watched as Lloyd ate like no human she had ever seen eat before. She picked at her meal, sipped her wine and smoked cigarettes while he made incredible amounts of food disappear. He paused only long enough to keep her glass filled.

"Drink up. Puts hair on your chest," Lloyd mumbled, wondering if there *was* hair on her chest like there was on her face. He told himself he'd find out before the night was through and returned his attention to the food still on the table. *First things first,* he thought, resuming his gluttony.

"So, why don't you tell me about your situation with your father and all," Lloyd said, reaching to fill her wine glass again with one hand while stuffing a biscuit into his mouth with the palm of his other.

"Drink up," he said again, and she did.

Shirley didn't know how long she had been watching Lloyd eat but she knew she was in awe of the performance. He had consumed no less than four pounds of meat so far and almost all of the cheese-smothered potatoes. Only two of the original twenty biscuits still remained uneaten and every last one of the malodorous Brussels sprouts was now somewhere in his digestive system. And he was showing no signs of even slowing down. Most of what was in Shirley's plate when she first sat down at the table was still untouched, the sweet, heavy wine having taken an early, appetite-curbing effect on her.

She was staring at the long ash at the end of the cigarette she held between her fingers wondering how much farther it could burn without falling off when she realized the room was spinning and Lloyd's words were now all but incomprehensible. She thought he was saying something about her father but she couldn't concentrate or make any sense of it. She tried to focus on Lloyd's face but found that to be impossible. She saw him pouring more wine from what looked like two bottles into two glasses. She felt one of her arms go limp and fall to her side. Shirley was vaguely aware of Lloyd taking the cigarette from her other hand and snuffing it out seconds before that arm also went limp. Lloyd was able to thrust his hand under Shirley's suddenly falling head, catching her face in his palm a split-second before it would have hit her plate of uneaten food. Her heavy head, like a dead weight, had sunk his puffy hand and fingers deep into the warm, gravy-covered meat and cheese-covered fries. He lifted her head and reached out to support her chin with his free hand, then began licking the gravy and cheese from his knuckles and from between his fingers. Lloyd then hoisted Shirley to her feet and half carried her to the couch in the next room. Seeing that some of the soft cheese had seeped through his fingers and now completely caked one of her eye sockets, he bent over her and licked that too.

Lloyd went back to the dining room and finished the last of the food in his plate and all that remained in the serving platters. He then ate what was in Shirley's plate too. He swabbed the remaining gravy and cheese with the last of the biscuits and, peering through the open doorway at the passed-out figure on the couch, opened another beer and drank it down. Lloyd then began belching like there was no tomorrow. Long, loud, groaning belches that soon gave way to a bout of flatulence not to be believed, probably the result of having wolfed down far too many Brussels sprouts. Lloyd would lean to one side, lifting one gargantuan buttock off the chair high enough to let the most horrendous fart imaginable escape his nether throat. He'd then lean the other way to lift the other cheek and expel another thunderous outburst. This vile scene continued for a good fifteen minutes, Lloyd swaying his massive torso from side to side, his fat, pimpled ass-cheeks alternately rising up in seeming competition with each other to aid and abet their owner in exuding his sickening supply of vulgar gas.

It wasn't the first time this act played out. It was a totally gross, but much-enjoyed ritual that Lloyd had perfected over many years of practice, although this was an unusually powerful episode and the first time he ever did it when he wasn't alone. Fortunately, Shirley was out cold. Fortunate not only because it spared her a despicable attack to her aural and olfactory senses, but because being the chain-smoker that she was, she undoubtedly would have tried lighting up, quite possibly blowing the gaseous room and everything in it to smithereens.

His tasteless theater having finally reached its closing act, Lloyd took a long gulp of beer, let loose one final burst of flatus and another burp, and then laboriously made his way into the next room. He walked over to the couch and there, within moments, conceived his first child with a still very drunk, semi-conscious Shirley Bershadski.

* * *

Shirley didn't wake up until very early the next morning. A more experienced drinker would have described what she was feeling as a *"wish-I-was-dead-hangover"* but this was the first hangover she ever had. Instead, she thought she *was* dead. She slowly raised herself up to a sitting position and tried to take in the scene. The pounding in her ears was deafening and a piercing pain was shooting through her head so fiercely that it brought tears to her eyes. Actually to one eye, the other being sealed shut with dried Cheese Whiz that managed to evade Lloyd's lapping tongue the previous night. She rose up from the couch and, taking baby steps, managed to inch her way into the dining room. Rubbing at her yet unopened eye, she succeeded in scraping away the cheese residue and surveyed the table. It was strewn with dishes, platters and utensils from last night's dinner. On her plate, which looked oddly as if it were licked clean, in fact *all* the plates looked that way, was a hand-written note. In nearly flawless and overly ornate penmanship it read:

Dearest Shirley—

It was a magnificent evening. You are a fine cook and a warm, generous lady who really knows how to treat a man. It's a damn shame that you were a little under the weather and thus unable to tell me all about your father's problems. I shall return when you're feeling better and you can try again. I suggest this coming Saturday. Same time, same place.

Lloyd Meshitsky, CPA
P.S. Don't bother changing the menu. It cannot be improved upon!

* * *

There followed over the next two months about a dozen or so more of these *dates* with little or no variation from the very first one. As instructed, Shirley never once varied the food, including the overdone slab of beef, although after time she began bringing it to the table unsliced, letting Lloyd butcher it even worse than she'd done. In fact, the only way these ensuing evenings differed at all was that Lloyd learned, little by little, just before Shirley's weekly muscatel-induced journeys into incoherent sexual passivity, everything he needed to know about her father Seth's medical and financial conditions, his real interest being only the latter of the two.

Shirley was an only child. Her mother had passed away four years earlier and for the past year, since her father had been diagnosed with cancer, she had been spending most of her time at his house in Fort Lee seeing to his needs. She spent so little time at her own apartment that, before Lloyd came on the scene, she had considered giving it up.

Seth was now confined to a hospital bed and Lloyd took advantage of his absence by spending his Sundays with Shirley at his vacant house, pouring over all of his records and financial documents dating back decades. He determined that as soon as old Seth took his last breath Shirley, as the sole beneficiary of his estate, would be sitting pretty. Her father owned two houses outright; the one in Fort Lee worth about $65,000; and a tiny, vacation cottage on Reach Island that, being located right on the water was worth at least that much or more. He owned stock worth approximately $85,000; had two life insurance policies, one for $50,000 and another worth $25,000. His car was worth about $3,500 and he kept a small boat at the shore that might fetch $5,000. He had $13,206 in a savings account and another $850 in personal checking. He had a modest income from the gas station in Fort Lee that he owned and operated for the last twenty-seven years which, since his illness, was now being run by his long time manager. Lloyd guessed it might be worth $80,000 to $100,000, maybe even more. Personal possessions amounted to another $7,000 or $8,000 so, all in all, Shirley would soon have a net worth of over four hundred thousand dollars. It caused Lloyd to salivate. Often to the point of dribbling.

His devious mind was working overtime hatching schemes to not only muscle in on this goldmine, but grow its value exponentially. These schemes ranged widely in both their form and their ethics. The best of them just smacked of utilizing highly questionable, morally objectionable tactics to the worst of them which were totally fraudulent and patently illegal.

Not once in her twenty-seven years had Shirley ever thought about her family assets, and certainly never knew they amounted to anything so substantial. The Bershadskis were just modest people leading modest lifestyles. Shirley herself had no experience with financial matters whatsoever. She could barely manage her own budget without advice and an occasional helping hand from her father.

So, when Lloyd told her she stood to inherit hundreds

of thousands of dollars she was overwhelmed with the news and completely clueless as to what to do. Precisely what Lloyd had predicted. And when he told her that if she didn't move fast the government would grab most of everything in taxes, leaving her with precious little she was terrified at the prospect. Again, precisely what Lloyd had predicted. And when he suggested that he be granted Power of Attorney over Seth's affairs to not only help her retain the bulk of her inheritance, but also to be able to act quickly to take advantage of opportunities that could further enhance her financial position, she bit like a hungry bluefish and Lloyd just effortlessly reeled her in. Precisely as expected.

Seth though, was another story. The plain truth was that he didn't like Lloyd one bit. He didn't like the way this accountant talked and he didn't trust him as far as he could throw him. The thought of frail, pain-ravaged Seth actually trying to *throw* Lloyd often brought a smile to the poor man's lips though, and Shirley and Lloyd both misread it simply as his being happy that they were there visiting him. Seth kept the real reason to himself. The more they continued to press their point about Power of Attorney the more Seth continued to resist the idea, so convinced was he that Shirley's new friend was nothing but bad news.

But Seth knew that he didn't have too much longer and he also knew that Shirley really *would* need someone's help with these matters and he promised himself that he would call his lawyer the very next day to enlist his assistance in that regard. When he finally did call him, though, it wasn't for the purpose he originally intended. He called and, with an occasional, barely audible sob in his voice, instructed his lawyer to draw up the papers that would grant Power of Attorney status over all of his affairs to one, Lloyd Meshitsky. That was five minutes after Shirley informed him that she was pregnant and that the slob would soon be his son-in-law.

Lloyd wasted no time at all after Seth signed the papers that gave him authority over his financial matters. He was a humongous mass of energy and evil intent, pausing only long enough to marvel at his amazing run of good fortune. In the span of little more than a year he went from being a brooding loner, stuck in a dreary dead-end job with a paltry salary to where he was today: A respected man with a business of his own, getting laid on a regular basis for the first time in his life without having to pay for it, soon to marry an adoring woman who was a terrific cook and, suddenly, a man with real assets about to embark on an entrepreneurial spree that could make him set for life.

Poor Seth descended into an ever-deepening state of depression soon after signing the document that officially transferred decision-making in his behalf over to Lloyd. Of course, he couldn't know exactly what Lloyd's plans were regarding his estate but his premonitions told him they would not be good. Three weeks later he died quietly in his hospital bed on the day of his daughter's courthouse wedding, at the precise moment Shirley said "*I do.*" He succumbed as much to the growing guilt he felt at inadvertently being responsible for all that lay ahead, as he did to the growing disease that relentlessly ravaged his body.

* * *

Sadly, Seth Bershadski never once even came *close* to resting in peace. Knowing that his daughter carried Lloyd's evil seed started him turning over in his grave the moment his casket was lowered into the ground. And five months later when Shirley gave birth to a son, his non-stop spinning went up a notch for this was a mean, hateful child and, despite Seth's unheard protestations, it was decided that the little bastard would be named after his dearly departed grandfather. The abhorrent conduct of his son-in-law and grandson would keep poor Seth spinning inside the cheap coffin that Lloyd selected, but never paid for, for the next eighteen years. Spinning out of control, like a supine Whirling Dervish.

J'net

Seems I was always the sort that tried seein' the good in people. And for the most part I could. Lookin' on the bright side of things instead of bellyachin' about this and squawkin' about that is a healthier way of goin' through life. At least it has been for me, anyway. Course, life's full of ups and downs for everybody but I always counted myself among the lucky ones, bein' blessed with three lovin' husbands and more wonderful friends than you could ever imagine. Dwellin' on the bad never does any good, that's been my motto. Life's too complicated as it is without tanglin' it up even more with needless negativity about things you can't do anything about anyway. Keep things simple is what I always say. I suppose that's what I liked most about Joe. He liked keepin' things simple too. Comes natural I guess if you're from Quaker stock. Joe never went overboard with anything. We had the things we needed and didn't want for anything we considered to be wasteful. Take Joe's boat for instance. He had more than enough money for something bigger and fancier but he was satisfied with the old wooden rowboat with that outboard motor of his. Never needed more for his purposes. Fishin' and crabbin' and clammin' is mostly all he used it for and it suited him just fine. Gave it a nice new paint job each spring and kept the motor tuned the way it should be. Course, all the neighbors had nicer boats for cruisin' around and water sports and such, that bein' a big part of their summer activity every year. I was always gettin' invited to go out on the bay with one or another of em but I'd generally decline. There was one time though when the DiMarcos and the Gorshins were goin' out for a sunset cocktail cruise on Spike and Jacko's boat and they talked us into joinin' em and I must say it was one of the nicest times we ever had. Even Joe admitted that bein' out on a pleasure boat was somethin' he might be able to get used to. Course, the Meshitsky boats were something else all together. Seems Lloyd got a new boat every year or two. And each one was bigger and louder than the one before. He even got his son a boat of his own when he was only about twelve. A noisy speedboat just like his father's, only smaller. That was the thing about the Meshitskys. Noise, noise and more noise. We called em the "loud family." Loud boats, loud cars, loud radios always blastin'. Even loud talkin'. Just sayin' something wasn't enough for em. It had to be said loud enough for the whole block to hear. Seems if they weren't constantly makin' a lot of noise they weren't happy. Sorta like they needed to be the focus of everybody's attention, always makin' sure that every little thing they did and every little thing they had would get noticed. And they had a lot and they kept gettin' more. Made sure to leave all their stuff strewn all over their yard and even on the property of their neighbors too. Ostentatious is what they were, all four of em, each in their own special way. Sorta sick if you ask me. Funny though, the way people would ignore most of it in the beginning and then slowly but surely, over several years actually, come to detest just about everything about em. Course, it took some longer than others to finally say they had enough of em. Little by little they'd start to grate on you and sooner or later you'd get to a point where you just couldn't take any more. Coincidentally, that was usually pretty soon after you realized you'd been bamboozled by Lloyd. And that included just about everyone. That's "Everyone" with a capital E.

Nine
Bunny. But of Course!

Lloyd had always been a liar, a sneak and a cheat. As a child he would steal money from his parents. He became good at shoplifting from stores. He'd steal toys and candy from other kids on a regular basis. Lloyd was a swine of a child disliked by everyone and, if not for his robust size even then, he surely would have been the boy who got beat up every day after school. His natural propensity for larceny had become such a part of his nature so early on that he had long ago stopped believing that it was even wrong. By the time Shirley and her dying dad entered his life he was more than ready to make the leap from being just a loathsome petty thief to a cunning, manipulative, totally contemptible prick of a man who, with his new-found resources, could be truly dangerous. About the only thing he lacked at this point was the brazenness and utter dismissal of normal human decency that would become his modus operandi in the years ahead.

Lloyd soon set about the business at hand, which began with establishing a labyrinth of dummy corporations designed to complicate anyone's efforts, should that ever occur, to track the movement of funds. It was an incredibly elaborate and effective smokescreen that included phony real estate holding companies, equipment leasing companies, petroleum companies, investment companies, consultancies and management companies. He set them up listing himself as chief executive of some, giving Shirley that title in others and even listing non-existing people as partners in still others. As seed money to start in motion some transactions that were a necessary prelude to a bigger plan down the road, he refinanced Seth's house in north Jersey just prior to his passing away for triple its actual value by providing the bank with an inflated appraisal prepared by his bogus real estate firm. He proceeded to never once make a single mortgage payment, forcing the bank to repossess the house long after Seth passed away; expressing to Shirley complete ignorance of a transaction that he professed was all her father's doing. The bank, unable to prove otherwise and deciding not to throw good money after bad with a costly, drawn-out lawsuit, took the hit as so many others would in the future. Lloyd then sold Seth's gas station business for a fraction of its value to his petroleum company, and he likewise sold for a song the land it was sitting on to his real estate company, which promptly sold it for even less to his investment firm. He then unceremoniously fired the gas station's long standing manager as well as its other employees, replacing them with illegal aliens at greatly reduced wages which allowed him to temporarily lower gas prices to a point where area competition could no longer survive. He then bought these suffering stations at distressed prices, convincing the sellers to accept small down payments and holding private mortgages themselves in order to recoup some of their losses in interest payments. Lloyd then would fail to make payments on the notes, forcing his creditors to begin legal actions which he would completely ignore, simply bankrupting the company being sued when judgments were granted, having long ago resold the stations and transferring any assets to his consulting company who, in a joint venture with his equipment leasing company, had leased the stations to shell corporations with off-shore bank accounts.

Lloyd then began relieving some of his doctor clients of what he believed to be their all-too-burdensome bank balances by convincing them that these gas stations would make perfect turn-key investments. The doctors trusted him enough to follow his advice and bought the stations at prices which, based on false balance sheets provided by Lloyd, might be considered high but not totally out of line. Based on Lloyd's recommendation, the doctors hired his management company to oversee the businesses and he would proceed to mismanage them for as long as could be gotten away with, until the stations themselves would be forced into bankruptcy having endured too many years of Lloyd's undetectable embezzlement. He'd then just start the process all over again, continuing to amass a considerable off-shore fortune.

At first Lloyd was astonished that he could actually get away with some of these things. But as time went on he simply told himself that he was smarter than everyone else, especially *those doctors* who, for the most part, would continue to be victims of his snow jobs even after their ventures had become financial disasters. And even those few who eventually were on to him never bothered to pursue matters beyond firing him as their accountant, probably too embarrassed at having been such easy touches. Lloyd didn't care at all when this happened because his CPA practice had become such an infinitesimal part of his income that he viewed it as little more than a vehicle to provide an unending supply of patsies. And since there was never a shortage of new doctors in the wings there was, likewise, never a shortage of new fish to fry.

Lloyd did not discriminate. It didn't matter if whatever it was that he was cheating someone out of or, in some cases, stealing, was big or small. Nor did it matter who the victim was. It might be a major financial institution, of which there were many, that should have known better but didn't. There were vendors of products or supplies for his businesses or even for his personal use who would go unpaid. And professional people like doctors and lawyers, and dozens of tradesmen of every kind over the years whose demands for payment he simply ignored. The theft of money, goods, services and labor all fit into the master plan, which was to keep the cash flowing in one direction and one direction only: Everything coming in and nothing, or as little as possible, going out. There came a time that Lloyd stopped paying for practically everything, including taxes of every kind, be they business or personal. Exceptions to this rule were those times when deposits or down payments were necessary in order to take possession of items of substance such as cars, boats or real estate. Lloyd always made sure these payments were as low as possible and in several instances actually stopped payment on checks before they cleared, often bringing frivolous, preemptive lawsuits against the other party for non-delivery or breach of contract. These cases would sometimes take years to resolve with Lloyd always retaining possession of, as well as having full use of, whatever was in dispute. Of course in the many instances where *Lloyd* was being sued, the cases would drag on and on, caused in part by a parade of new defense attorneys, each replacing a previous one who had not been paid, and who by that time might also be suing Lloyd. So, for the most part, anyone attempting legal action against him usually ended up wasting even more time and money with very disappointing results. The majority would finally give up after being frustrated for months or years of watching the painfully slow and expensive legal process take its toll on them. Those few that did persevere would ultimately win their cases but would also learn that it was one thing to win a judgment in court but quite another to actually collect on it. Lloyd would always be one step ahead of them and manage to close bank accounts before they could be levied upon and strip the defending companies of any tangible assets prior to being seized. That he continued his behavior without ever being scathed was almost beyond belief. Each successful scam served to reinforce and increase Lloyd's already inflated sense of superiority over others and resulted in even bolder and more contemptible conduct on his part.

Shirley meanwhile, never once asked Lloyd anything about financial matters. She was convinced that he was a genius with money. The changes to her lifestyle that began taking place were just too great for any other explanation. She simply never gave it a thought and, instead, busied herself getting used to the latest material acquisition that came their way. *Conspicuous consumption* was a term that Shirley had never heard and never would, yet it was a term that would come to be defined by the Meshitskys over the next two decades.

But in truth, Shirley never became totally comfortable with her new life. In fact, she spent those next decades trying without much success to stop feeling like the trespasser that she was in a world where she did not belong. Sophistication of any sort simply did not reside in the Meshitsky household. It didn't automatically come with the materialistic values that were to govern their very existence. And regardless of the apparent wealth they so desperately sought to project, it was impossible to mask the truth for very long. Anyone having more than a fleeting acquaintance with them soon learned, many at great cost, that the Meshitskys' entire existence, notwithstanding outward appearances, was a total fraud and any possessions they had were likely ill-gotten. It was a fraud masterminded by Lloyd of course, but it was one that his family would willingly buy into, somehow knowing about but never admitting, not even to themselves, the wretchedness that was at their core. They each relished the lifestyle and ever-increasing amount of *stuff* that was a part of it too much to care much about how it was coming their way. In fact, so insulated were they by the maze created by Lloyd that his activities rarely ever affected them personally, and when they did it amounted to little more than an occasional inconvenience. Changing their already unlisted phone numbers or darkening the house and pretending no one was home if someone resembling a process server approached became a natural part of their lives. It was a small price to pay considering what they were getting in return, and Lloyd had convinced them that winning in business sometimes required such measures. Over time, a *"them against us"* mentality had become instilled in all of their minds and they actually came to believe that the things they sometimes heard people say about Lloyd and, by extension, about themselves as well, was just pure envy at their family's obvious success.

* * *

Shirley would give birth to a second child, a girl, just eleven months after Seth was born. Not yet having decided on a name, Lloyd and Shirley watched her through the glass as she slept along with the other infants in the hospital's maternity ward and discussed some possibilities. The baby's nose would begin twitching every few minutes prompting Shirley to say, "Lloyd, did you see that? She looks like a little bunny."

"Bunny. *But of course!* Bunny will be her name!" Lloyd bellowed, startling Shirley along with everyone else in the hospital corridor. As if hearing her name for the first time through the thick glass, the baby began twitching her nose repeatedly as her father urged her on, roaring with laughter.

It wasn't exactly the kind of name Shirley had in mind but it seemed to thrill Lloyd no end, so she just shrugged her shoulders and thought well, *why not?* They became so enamored with the cuteness of how Bunny got her name that, thereafter, they never failed to tell it every chance they could, usually more than once, to everyone they'd ever meet. And of course they would always make little Bunny re-enact the precious event each time.

"Bunny, show Mr. and Mrs. So-and-So how you got your name" they would say to her. And Bunny would happily respond by scrunching up her face and twitching her nose to the unending delight of her parents and the polite tolerance of everyone else. Except for her brother Seth, who wanted to puke every time he'd witness the insipid scene.

Bunny turned out to be a surprisingly harmless individual considering her immediate stock. She wasn't mean-spirited like her brother. She lacked the desire to take advantage of others that was so prevalent in Lloyd and in Seth too. She basically went through every day wishing no ill will toward anyone, a trait probably handed down from the grandfather she never knew. Like her mother, she wasn't all that brilliant but she *was* smart enough to notice some of what transpired around her and was cognizant of what people would sometimes be saying. And the older she got the more things she got wind of. There was no question that her brother was vile to the bone. She couldn't even remember a single time in her life that he was anything but downright nasty toward her. And of course she couldn't help hearing the way some people talked about her father. Maybe certain things they said were true and maybe they weren't. But if these things bothered her at all she never showed any outward signs of it. Perhaps she felt as helpless as poor old Seth, six feet under, powerless to do anything about anything. Or perhaps she was like her mother, not only refusing to do anything that might rock the boat, but actually turning a blind eye to the real truth, denying it even to herself, in order to maintain the good life.

*   *   *

In the early spring of 1982, after having spent ten summers in the little cottage once owned by the long dead Seth Bershadski, Lloyd decided it was time to move on to something bigger and better. The bayfront cottage had more than served its purpose. Shirley and the kids had a great time every year. And Lloyd had really gotten into boating in a big way. So much so that his plans for three new boats—a big, powerful, thirty-one foot Scarab that he'd already picked out for himself; a nimble, smaller version along the same lines for his eleven-year-old son Seth; and maybe a nice little sailboat for his daughter Bunny—were beyond the mooring capacity of the little property with its meager dock. Besides, Lloyd believed that the South Beach section of the Reach wasn't good enough for the Meshitskys any longer. A classier place was long overdue. Plus, their relationship with the neighbors was becoming more and more strained with each passing day. Ed Wood, his neighbor on the right, had accused Seth of stealing tools from his garage and was saying as much to anyone who'd listen. Bill and Marilyn Elkton, on the left, had begun to suspect the same when things started to disappear from their place too. Marilyn had stopped talking to Shirley altogether. Lloyd convinced Shirley that she was just jealous of the big diamond ring that he'd given her recently and told her she'd have to get used to inferior people being envious of her. Shirley of course believed him as she believed everything Lloyd said. But that had nothing at all to do with it. The real reason was that by this time Lloyd had totally stopped caring about who his victims were and

Bill Elkton was slowly becoming aware that he was being royally screwed by his neighbor and supposed friend of almost a decade.

Lloyd had recently begun combining convenience stores into some of his gas stations and had hired Elkton, who was an architect, to plan the additions to three of the locations. That was almost two years ago and, instead of seeing a cent of the nine thousand dollars owed him, all he got from Lloyd was excuses, promises and more excuses. And that wasn't the only thing making life at the shore uncomfortable for Lloyd. The cottage had long ago been sold to one of Lloyd's shell corporations and the Meshitskys had been living in it rent free for years. The company had fraudulently taken out three different mortgages totaling almost four times the actual value of the property and the proceeds of these loans quickly disappeared into Lloyd's maze-like laundering apparatus, eventually finding its way into an off-shore numbered bank account in Central America. And since mortgage or real estate tax payments hadn't been made for quite some time it was highly unlikely that they could get through another season without a foreclosure and seizure so, all things considered, it was indeed a good time to move on. Shirley and the kids conducted a yard sale during the off season selling everything that wasn't nailed down and, since their immediate neighbors weren't around, it included a trove of items stolen from them by Seth over the years.

Lloyd had only one other thing from their years at the cottage in South Beach to dispose of before beginning life anew at the fine house they found in Bayberry that winter. That was his old boat, which he deemed far too pedestrian and no longer befitting his position and soon-to-be new environment of Bay Vista. Not to mention the fact that the sheriff was about to seize it for the bank that had financed it.

Having insured it for twice what he could ever sell it for Lloyd made sure to keep up with the premiums for just the right time, which had now arrived. So, on the first spring-like day of 1983, he and Seth drove it up to a desolate lagoon in Dune City and scuttled it. It would be months before that part of the Island started to come alive again, and it wouldn't be discovered until long after he collected on his claim.

J'net

I can remember the very first block party like it was yesterday. Back in '83, that first summer. Course, it wasn't called a block party that year, just a big birthday party for the three girls. To this day I still wonder if the good Lord made those families have kids on the same day and sorta guided them all to Bay Vista in the first place just so there'd be an excuse for the big season-endin' festivities. Well, why not I always said. Joe always chuckled every time I'd proffer that idea. Anyway, there was a big crowd even back then. Seems everybody had friends and relatives there and other people who lived nearby were also part of the big night. Day and night I should say cause it always started pretty early in the afternoon. At least for those on Bay Vista it did. First the cocktails and finger food and then the serious gourmet food would make its way down to the stones. My, I don't know where they learned to cook like that. Course, they each had their own specialties, mostly family favorites and that's what they made for the party. And it evolved from there, gettin' better and better every year though every year you'd swear it couldn't get any better. There seemed to be a never-endin' supply of recipes each one had and they really relished in showin' them off. Except for the Meshitskys. Shirley'd make the same damn thing year after year. First clams casino. Then London broil. I thought the clams were always pretty good. Joe wouldn't go near any of their stuff that first year or any year. Course, for him, with good reason I was still to learn. The beef wasn't up to snuff though. Not like the dishes from the other kitchens, that's for sure. Lloyd kept sayin' it was filet mignon and Jacko would always correct him. Year after year. Then one year Seth was mad at Shirley for some reason and he let on that she didn't make the clams herself. Seems they found an Eye-talian restaurant on the mainland that made up a big platter of em every year. And they never let on it wasn't Shirley's. The London broil was all hers though. "Combat boot leather" is how Max Gorshin described it that first year and that's what it was called all the years thereafter. Behind their backs of course. I never saw anybody except Lloyd eat it. Most times all of it too. I remember how Lloyd told all the new people there that night how he was a CPA and kept showin' everyone, me included, his damn numbers conundrum over and over till we couldn't take it any more. He never stopped in all the years since, either. And I believe that evenin' was the first time Seth started cacklin' like a seagull though nobody knew it was him at the time cause he kept outa sight when he was doin' it. Got to be pretty annoyin' as I recall. Out of place too, cause it was nighttime and gulls are usually quiet at night, but I guess nobody was payin' that close attention to it. A little nerve-rackin' though is how I remember it. But, as annoyin' as it was I guess I'd have to say he got pretty good at it. The birds made different kinda sounds too and the nasty little nuisance had em all down pat. And oh my, the wines! Joe and I sure got ourselves quite an education on good wines over the years at the block parties. "Enlightened palates" is how Jacko termed what it was we were developin'. And I have to admit he was right. We never thought of wine as somethin' so special before but when you start tastin' the good ones there's no goin' back. Anyway, the parties sorta had a certain personality all their own and I guess it started with that very first one. Wonderful food. Wonderful wines. Gaiety and conviviality among most everyone. Seth generally bein' a pain in the ass one way or another. Shirley tryin' to find a way to fit in. Lloyd takin' his noisy boat out for a five-minute spin around sunset just to bring it right back and practically givin' everybody a headache doin' it. Joe steerin' clear of the Meshitskys. Grown people jumpin' in the bay fully clothed at midnight. Me marvelin' at it all. Can't really remember when some of the quirkiness in a few of the people started to become apparent, though. Maybe that first year, maybe later. The best was Harry Elias. He and his wife Molly owned one of the interior houses across the road on Bay Vista. Seems if he got a few drinks in him he turned into a bona fide kleptomaniac. I remember the first time anybody noticed it. He started takin' stuff back to his house. Dumb stuff like some plastic forks. Or a couple of pastries. Even a loaf of Mona's garlic bread. He'd just saunter off with things and come back and grab somethin' else. When he got found out, Jacko had to scold him. And poor Molly, she was a weeper. She'd weep every time he got caught. If you ask me I don't even think he knew he was doin' it. Sorta out of his control. Anyway, the other men would draw straws each year and the loser would have to keep an eye on Harry and politely stop him before he'd disappear with whatever he was takin'. And poor Molly would start weepin' again. It was Shirley who usually tried to comfort her. When all was said and done I guess Shirley didn't really have a bad heart when it came to things like that. Just a bad husband. And a bad son. Anyway, the parties would go on without ever skippin' a beat. It was years until I started to notice a little uneasiness creepin' in among certain people regardin' the Meshitskys. Course, Joe was uneasy from day one. Other than him I believe it was Marco who first showed signs of it. Then maybe the doctors, Max and Rich. Course, toward the end it was just about everyone who displayed some tenseness when it came to Lloyd. That's "Tenseness" with a capital T.

Ten
Opie's on the Case!

There was no such thing as "the other side of the tracks" on the Reach. There was *the other side of the bay.* If you were to travel westward far enough on that side of the bay, perhaps forty or fifty miles, into what was known as "*the Bogs*" you would find yourself in an area of dense marshland with permanently wet and spongy ground, decaying plants, trees and foliage that never seem to grow or die, all manner of insects and an amazing array of unusual wildlife. Encompassing an area of more than a hundred square miles, it is flush in bog iron deposits, formed by iron oxide-rich waters flowing over peat soils. Bog iron is perhaps the first iron mined by humans, notably early Vikings, and is the only self-replenishing source of the mineral. The Bogs, and areas like it, were once an important supplier of the nation's first iron production, used for tools and munitions. Today it is an area that is sparsely populated by a subculture of human inhabitants that somehow manage to thrive in that harsh environment. In some respects they are people probably not unlike those in rural, mountainous Appalachia whose families date back countless generations and are content with keeping things exactly as they are. "*Boggies.*" That's what they call themselves and that's how everyone else refers to them too when they encounter them. Which isn't all that often as they rarely venture outside of their vast, cloistered habitat if not absolutely necessary. Not overly friendly, not overly clean, self-schooled, self-reliant and likely with a fair amount of inbreeding going on, they are set in their ways and frown on becoming too involved with the outside world. The men are usually bearded, hard-drinking, tough-looking, and the women aren't much softer. With few exceptions, kids share in the adults' disdain of anything foreign to their normal, ordered way of life. One such exception was Butchie Turloch. Butchie wanted more, straying outside of the Bogs frequently. And when Butchie met Seth Meshitsky and saw what he had, he decided he wanted a lot more.

In most ways the two boys couldn't be less alike. Seth, tall, blonde,tan and athletic looking. And spoiled beyond words with more of everything than any kid ever needed or deserved. Butchie, shorter, husky, with oily, black curly hair and a sickly like, pimpled pallor. Dirt poor, street smart and cunning. They had only two things in common: Their age, which was fourteen when they met, and a pre-programmed mean streak that bordered on the sadistic, which seemed to govern their very existence. Two malignant peas in a pod that hit it off immediately which didn't bode well for those around them.

Hanging around with Seth was like dying and going to heaven for Butchie. By the time their second summer season together rolled around Butchie was practically living in the Meshitsky household and that was bad news for most people at Bay Vista, none more so than for Bunny. Seth was never nice to his sister and pretty much ignored her his whole life. At fourteen Bunny was fairly well-developed physically and, feeding off his new friend's prurient tendencies, Seth's indifference toward her was replaced with creepy, menacing, sexually implicit mental abuse. Butchie was just hell-bent on terrorizing her with a relentless salaciousness that knew no bounds. Together, Seth and Butchie made life fairly miserable for Bunny and for most of her friends too.

Bunny's complaints to her mother usually fell on deaf ears. Shirley had long ago thrown up her hands and stopped being a responsible parent where Seth's behavior was concerned and had relinquished any disciplinary duties to Lloyd, whose bark always turned out to be bigger than his bite. Threats of being grounded or punishment of any kind were empty ones, forgotten as soon as Lloyd uttered them. In fact, the Meshitskys' parenting skills were so lacking that Seth's disrespect for both of them, especially Shirley, was openly displayed. It was evident for all to see far too often and, in time, a topic of conversation among neighbors. As far as anyone knew, there were only two occasions when Lloyd actually followed through on a promised punishment. The first was when he found Seth and Butchie huddled in Seth's darkened bedroom closet. At some point Seth apparently had calculated that his closet was directly above the outdoor shower located under the house and had bored a three-quarter inch hole through the fiber board flooring and then through the plywood below it. One day Lloyd thought he heard noises coming from the closet and had caught them. Evidently, they were taking turns at watching one of Bunny's friends as she showered who, upon hearing Lloyd's yelling and the scuffling noises coming from above, looked up and noticed the hole and started screaming like a banshee. Seth was grounded for a week with Butchie banned from visiting him.

The fact that Butchie's bathing trunks were down around his knees and Seth's were off completely when the closet door opened was never given a second thought by Lloyd who had long ago stopped copulation with Shirley in favor of ritualistic, thrice-weekly maniacal masturbation in the privacy of his giant Jacuzzi. He'd immerse himself in the turbulent water with lustful visions of his most recently encountered comely woman amid stacks and stacks of money and gently swaying palm trees somewhere in Belize. So, naturally, he assumed that what they were doing in the closet was what he often did in the Jacuzzi. Certainly understandable in Lloyd's opinion for two boys peeping at a real live naked girl below. But, unknown to Lloyd, the naked girl was only half the story. Less than half, actually.

As was usually the case, Seth's transgressions were soon forgotten and his sentence lasted only two days.

Not knowing how long the spying had been going on, or the number of victims, poor Bunny and all of her friends were forever mortified. Especially as Seth and Butchie never missed an opportunity to remind them of the incident with sneers, leers and snide remarks about various parts of their anatomy.

The second time Seth was punished was a lot worse. Worse because, in Lloyd's eyes, the crime was disgraceful beyond reproach or even imagination. This time Seth's penalty would be severe. And this time exacting it would be something Lloyd would come to regret. As would all of his neighbors.

It was the end of the '87 season. People were readying their homes for the winter, storing away anything that might be damaged by the brutal off-season weather to come. Lloyd was busy making room in the shed for the outdoor furniture and other summer items when he moved a large bin away from the back wall and found a bag filled with a stack of magazines and a bunch of Polaroid snapshots. He took some out and froze, not believing his eyes. Lloyd dropped them, stormed out to where Seth was hosing down his Jet Ski, grabbed him by the hair and dragged him, kicking and screaming, back to the shed. Releasing his grip on Seth's shock of hair he stared at his son with pure hatred in his bulging eyes, red-faced by the blood rushing into his head, his veins ready to explode.

"You're a goddamn faggot!" he said, half hissing, half growling.

Seth, scared and speechless, looked away from his enraged giant of a father to the pile of pornographic evidence strewn on the floor and looked back in time to see Lloyd's fist a split second before it landed squarely on his nose, spewing blood all over both of them and sending Seth crashing into a pile of beach chairs.

Lloyd turned and started walking out and, as he did, Seth heard him say, "That's it. Say goodbye to your boat. Goddamn faggot!"

* * *

From the very beginning Lloyd and Seth had a special relationship. Certainly not one that would ever earn Lloyd *"Father of the Year"* status, but special nonetheless. Seth was the one Lloyd actually confided in and would boast to, even as a young child. He let Seth in on just enough of his larceny over the years to instill a sick sort of respect for himself in the eyes of the boy. And the more he told him the greater their camaraderie grew. Seth was truly in awe of his father's propensity for wrongdoing and emulated him with a natural, inherited ease. As time went on Lloyd hinted that they were getting close to *"dropping out."* Spurred on by his son's seemingly unabashed hero-worship, Lloyd took pride in explaining that that was what he called his "master plan." It meant that they would finally have enough money someday to be able to just disappear to another part of the world where it would be summer all year long and they'd never have to work another day in their lives. He bragged that he'd been stashing a lot of money away in a safe place where no one would ever be able to find it. He bragged that they'd soon be really rich without a trouble in the world. And he swore Seth to secrecy, telling him he was the only person on earth who knew anything about the plan. Seth of course was pumped up with the self-importance this implied and with the trust his father obviously had in him. He relished hearing about each new scam Lloyd got away with and how much money it would contribute to their hidden *dropout cache*. After a while they developed a way of talking in a kind of code that no one else was privy to. Lloyd let Seth in on just about everything in his scheme, including the timing of the final act or, as he called it with a wink of his eye, *D-day*. Seth would smugly return the wink, cognizant of the fact that he was the only one in the family that knew that D-day meant *dropout* day. That day was only a couple of years away, as Lloyd estimated. About the only details Lloyd refused to reveal to Seth, no matter how many times he asked, were where the money was and what part of the world they were headed for to start a new life.

* * *

The camaraderie that had built up over the years between Lloyd and Seth dissipated like a balloon suddenly losing its air. *Whoosh.* Gone, never to return. The winter following the incident in the shed was hell for Seth. Lloyd hardly acknowledged his existence and barely spoke a word to him. Shirley and Bunny were clueless as to the reason and Lloyd was as tightlipped as could be, refusing at first to even admit there was a problem and finally forbidding any discussion about it whatsoever. Seth was sullen and morose and equally silent on the subject. Bunny, at the beginning, was glad Seth was in trouble but after a while even she began to feel a little sorry for Seth. Never had Lloyd been so mad for so long. At anyone or anything. Shirley decided that whatever happened was beyond her control so she ignored it like she ignored most things.

Seth kept hoping it would blow over like everything else always did. When they were alone a few times he lamely tried denying what Lloyd accused him of, saying that he was only holding the magazines for Butchie, but that was only half true and Seth was a bad liar when it came to lying to his father. There was no deceiving the master of deceit. Plus, there was no explaining the pictures. He tried saying he'd had girlfriends, which was true enough, although none ever lasted too long. Lloyd, in a rare talkative mood, once responded by saying that he now knew why they didn't stick around. Seth welcomed the remark because at least it meant his father was talking to him. Which was a good sign, surely meaning the whole mess would soon be a thing of the past. Seth spent a lot of time alone that winter trying to assure himself that everything would be back to normal by springtime, which was all that mattered. But he was wrong, even though in *his* mind his father seemed more at ease in his presence.

Seth was yet to turn seventeen and, in truth, he didn't think of himself as being gay. He kept telling himself this was all Butchie's fault. Butchie was into anything, especially if there was money in it. The two of them occasionally went up to Dune City and took the horny, generous queers for whatever they could, which was usually nothing to sneeze at. If any Polaroids were taken, which was sometimes the case during their capricious escapades, they'd always make sure they had them before they left the homes of their "*marks,*" as they were called. They should have burned them, but they saved them for no apparent reason other than that they were good for some laughs when they were bored. And they would take other things too if they thought they could sell them. And fruity porno magazines just for the hell of it. Good for more laughs.

But he kept telling himself that none of that meant he was gay. Just a dabble here and there, and only for a few kicks, and to squeeze whatever could be squeezed from some of the up-Island queers. But even that rationale would never fly with Lloyd, so homophobic was he. The very *idea* of anything homosexual was revolting to him, and he made no secret of the fact that he'd rather his son was a murderer or a rapist or anything else other than a goddamn *faggot*.

"I am not a fag. I am not a fag. I am not a fag." Seth would say those words over and over and over that winter. Never out loud, only to himself. Like when he was younger, in school, and was made to write "*I will not talk in class*" on the chalk board a hundred times. Two hundred times. You paid for the infraction and, *poof,* it would be over. Problem solved.

Curiously, or, more accurately, amazingly, the Father Kev stuff never even entered his thought process during this period. Not even once. If no one knew, then it didn't exist. Not caught, not a problem.

* * *

The Meshitskys were always the first family in Bay Vista to return to the Reach each spring. Usually weeks before everyone else who customarily waited until Memorial Day to open up their houses for the season. The first order of business for Lloyd was always to get his boat into the water and ready for operation and this year would be no different. Most years meant at least one brand new boat, a bigger and more powerful one, would be moored at the Meshitsky dock, taking the place of a previous one that had gone the way of a creditor's seizure. This season Lloyd's new toy was a monster of a speed machine. Forty feet long and powered by three terrifyingly loud engines, it dwarfed the dock it was tied to by almost ten feet. Like every one of Lloyd's boats before it, both sides of its long, sleek hull was emblazoned in fiery red italic lettering with the same old boring, pompous, ostentatious name: *"CPA EXPRESS."*

Lloyd's plan for the next winter season was to try his luck at off-shore power boat racing down in Florida. He'd been toying with the idea for some time and the idea itself had actually given way to a scam that had already produced a pretty penny for his long-range master plan. Still a fledging sport, the only prerequisite its participants were required to have was enough money or enough financial backing to be able to afford a boat worthy of competition, and the continuing resources necessary to fund competing on the circuit. Lloyd now had such a boat. At least for the time being. Keeping it, and dealing with the rest of the details still needed some work. And a new patsy.

Seth couldn't be more excited at the prospect of Lloyd's racing activities and what it might mean for himself. But, at the same time, he couldn't be more worried. They were back on speaking terms to some extent although Lloyd was a different person toward him. It was like an invisible wall was now between them that all but prevented the fellowship that once existed from being exhibited. The joking, winking, *partners-in-crime* aspect of their relationship was gone, replaced with an uncaring coldness on Lloyd's part that actually concerned Seth who normally wasn't concerned with anything. He hoped this too would eventually dissipate, as did Lloyd's earlier period of treating him as if he didn't even exist. Surely it would, he kept telling himself, and stopped worrying about it, preferring instead to think ahead to what would definitely be the most exciting of all winters. Skipping school was already a foregone conclusion in his mind. He'd be way too busy in Florida helping to crew the boat. He was already thinking of ways to get Butchie involved. That would really be a gas. He pictured being right at his father's side, the co-pilot or maybe the throttle man, a key member of the team that would take every checkered flag. Things between them would be back to normal in no time. He was sure of it. But first things first he told himself. For now let's just try to have a blast this summer. He didn't know it yet but he was in for a rude awakening.

It was now their third weekend at the shore and Seth's boat was yet to make its appearance, which was understandable. Lloyd's fabulous new boat took priority this year, as it should. But that was getting to be old news now and Seth was anxious to see his own powerful pride and joy again. A long, swift, beauty of a catamaran with engines almost as fierce as Lloyd's. Brand new last season and hardly broken in yet, it was much too much boat for most people and Seth couldn't wait to get it out on the bay once more.

That night at dinner he started to tease Lloyd, saying, but not really believing, that his *WILD CAT* could run circles around the new *CPA EXPRESS*. Lloyd just kept eating, ignoring the comment, ignoring its speaker.

Bunny answered for him. "No way. Dad's new boat would destroy yours."

"Shut up, rabbit puss. Nobody's talking to you."

"Mom!"

"Don't call her that" Shirley said, without much conviction.

"You shut up too. I wasn't talking to you either."

"Lloyd!"

Lloyd continued eating, not interested at the moment in being part of what passed for normal dinner conversation in the Meshitsky household.

Seth pressed on. "Come on, Dad, ten bucks says *the Cat* can outrun you."

Lloyd ladled more of Shirley's frankfurter stew onto his plate, grabbed another slice of Wonder bread from his evening's personal loaf and resumed eating in silence.

"*I'll* take that bet," Bunny said smugly.

"Blow me, rodent nose."

"Mom! . . . Dad!"

"Stop your cursing and finish your dinner," Shirley admonished him.

"*Blow's* not a curse word, Einstein."

"Lloyd!"

Again, not a word from Lloyd, his concentration on trying not to drip any gravy from the slice of sopping bread he'd just dunked, knuckle-deep, into the stewpot before it could reach his mouth.

"Mom said finish your dinner," Bunny said with a faint smile, knowing the dish wasn't one of Seth's favorites.

"You finish it, mousemaid," Seth sneered as he reached across with his plate, dumping its contents into hers as well as on the table all around it, adding "Tastes like pigmy shit if you ask me. Looks like it too."

"You're disgusting!" Bunny screamed, folding her arms and looking to her parents for help. Shirley just sighed and shook her head. Lloyd kept eating.

Feeling in control now, Seth started goading Lloyd. "What's the matter, Dad, afraid you'll lose ten bucks?"

No response.

"Tell you what. We'll make it a gentlemen's bet. I know I can take you. You know it too. I'll prove it too, as soon as *the Cat's* tuned up and back in the water."

Lloyd wiped his mouth, drained a can of beer, let out a belch that lasted a good five seconds and stared across at Seth. It was the first time he looked his son squarely in the eye in seven months. He let out another belch. Not quite as long as the first one, but louder. That was Bunny's cue. She knew the farting wasn't far behind so she retreated over into the living room area, which was part of the open, first floor space, and plopped on the sofa.

Seth, no longer accustomed to meeting Lloyd's gaze, much less his unrelenting stare, felt suddenly uncomfortable, knowing his control of matters, so strong just a moment ago was now very definitely ebbing. And his father was yet to say a word. The unusual silence in the room was perplexing to Shirley, made evident by her frown. Bunny, over in the living room, grabbed a pillow and clutched it to her bosom and watched the scene, sensing something momentous was imminent.

Seth broke the painful silence saying a little too matter-of-factly and a little too flippantly, "So when's my boat going back in the water?"

Never had anyone in the family ever heard Lloyd speak so softly or so slowly before. His eyes still fixed on Seth, he said, "You-don't-*have*-a-boat. I sold it."

Shirley's mouth dropped. Bunny's mouth dropped. They were both bug-eyed, not comprehending Lloyd's words. Seth wasn't bug-eyed. His eyes were slowly closing to the point of being slithers. Menacing, hateful slithers staring back at his father as the meaning of what he heard began to sink in.

Seth never thought for a moment that his father meant what he said in the shed last year. Never once. Why should he have? He was always able to get around any trouble he'd gotten into before. Why was this so different? The full impact of his not having his boat—*his* boat—for the season was impossible to fathom. That boat *was* the season. He was the envy of every kid on the Island. Grown-ups too. This couldn't be happening. He couldn't *let* it happen. His fists were clenched so tight they began to throb.

Lloyd had a feeling that Seth treated the episode in the

shed as insignificant and his promised punishment as an empty threat. Now, seeing him sitting there, he was sure of it and Lloyd was actually relishing every second of the torment visible on the face of his son. His *former* son, he corrected himself, as there wasn't an ounce of compassion left in him for the boy. He was still living under his roof but Seth was dead to him. He could stay or he could leave tomorrow. Lloyd really didn't care one way or the other. From the moment he found that bag in the shed and saw what was inside, Lloyd simply turned the page on Seth. Closed the book, in fact, as he no longer had any relevance in his life as far as Lloyd was concerned. He was a little surprised that Seth didn't know it until now. And he *did* know it now. The hatred in his eyes said it all. Lloyd returned his look of hatred with one of antipathy and disgust.

"YOU FUCKING MOTHERFUCKING BASTARD FUCK! IT WAS *MY* FUCKING BOAT YOU FUCKING SONOFABITCH! *MY* FUCKING BOAT! YOU HAD NO RIGHT YOU FUCKING PRICK! I HOPE YOU FUCKING DIE! YOU'LL PAY FOR THIS YOU FAT FUCKING MOTHERFUCKING COCKSUCKING SCUMBAG! I FUCKING HATE YOU! I FUCKING HATE ALL OF YOU!"

Seth's sudden ranting and raving scared the living hell out of Shirley who ran into the kitchen and grabbed a frying pan in case Seth tried attacking her. Bunny started wailing, trying to cover her eyes and ears at the same time and failing at both. Barney jumped up from his doggie-dream and began howling like never before. Lloyd was glued to his seat, one eye on Seth as he flailed his arms and kicked furniture in a wild, spitting, screaming, cursing dance around the room. All the while Lloyd had his other eye on a knife near his plate just in case Seth tried something stupid.

The raging stopped as suddenly as it started with Seth storming out and jumping into his car. At least he still had *it*.

He started it up and gunned the engine, tearing out of Bay Vista in a cloud of dust and making a skidding, screeching, two-wheeled turn onto the street, just missing hitting the split-rail fence in front of the Cooper house where Joe and J'net were enjoying their sunset cocktails, scaring the living hell out of them too.

Seth roared onto the Boulevard making another two-wheeled turn and raced his black Porsche convertible onto the causeway leading off of the Reach and didn't slow down until he was deep into the Bogs. He found Butchie at his favorite hang-out and the two of them spent the rest of the night plotting an alcohol-affected revenge.

* * *

Three days later, at four P.M. on the Wednesday before the big Memorial Day weekend, on orders from Detective Sergeant Stanley "Opie" Opelenczcic, Desk Officer Warren Blankfeld of the Bayberry Police Department began making the first of his five phone calls to the bayfront homeowners of the development known as Bay Vista. The numbers were obtained from the borough's Town Hall, where the emergency contact information of all absentee property owners was on file. He reached the Drakes and the Gorshins in Philadelphia, Irene Drake at her residence and Dr. Max Gorshin at his office. He spoke to Sharon Kosciusko at her home in Cherry Hill and Lloyd Meshitsky at his home in Watchung. He found Mona DiMarco at her husband's office in Manhattan. He informed each of them that there had been an incident of vandalism involving their homes and asked that someone in each household come down to assess the damage to their property and make an inventory of their possessions to determine what, if anything, might be missing. They all promised to be there early the very next day.

Earlier that day Officer Blankfeld was one of three Bayberry police officers—there were only five in the entire borough—on the scene with Detective Opelenczcic helping to conduct the investigation. While there he interviewed Joe and J'net Cooper and took their statements which, in his opinion, provided as strong a lead as anyone could hope for. Officer Blankfeld thanked them and made an attempt to ease the obvious and certainly very understandable concern he saw on the faces of the Coopers. Stuff like this just wasn't something that was supposed to happen on the Reach. It was definitely the biggest thing to happen since he'd been on the force.

He glanced over at his superior who, until that day, hadn't investigated anything more serious than a stolen bike or a drunk driving fender-bender. The detective was barking orders and scurrying here, there, everywhere, and then back again all over the property, running in and out of each house, taking pictures, frantically making notes of anything and everything. A man possessed.

Officer Blankfeld nodded toward his boss and proudly told them, "Not to worry, folks. Opie's on the case."

To which Joe replied, "Yeah. That's what I'm afraid of."

* * *

From that day on life on Bay Vista was never the same. The case was never officially solved, except in the minds of the residents. The fervor exhibited by Detective Opie Opelenczcic that first day inexplicably disappeared within twenty-four hours. The case was put on the back burner, where it remains to this day.

J'net

I swear, the way that car took the turn off of Bay Vista's little unpaved road where it intersected with the eastbound street it's a miracle it didn't flip over right onto our porch. That damn kid is gonna kill somebody some day. I thought Joe was gonna have himself a heart attack for sure. Scared us half to death. We had to have ourselves a second scotch that night just to calm down. Shouldn't let kids that age drive alone anyway if you ask me, especially as the sunlight was practically gone too. That one's a real menace to society. First with his damn boat and now with his damn car. Things were bad enough with that boy before he had em. Lethal weapons is what they are. And two days later, just about the time we put the incident out of our minds, he goes and pulls the same stunt all over again. This time in the middle of the night. Course, it was a lot darker and I was only able to get a glimpse of the car but it was the same shape and black, with the top down and the screeching noise it made roundin' the corner was identical to the one before and I'd swear on a stack of Bibles it was him again. And he wasn't alone this time. Who else would be tearin' out of Bay Vista like a madman anyway? None of the other families were even down as yet this year anyway. Yeah, it was him all right. Most likely with that weird lookin' pal of his. And I told that to the police. And when some of the folks came down the next day I told them too. What a mess. Funny, if the wind wasn't howlin' the way it was that night and blowin' south away from our place maybe we would've heard some of the destruction better, or earlier, in time for them to get caught but we didn't. We weren't even sure we were hearin' anything but the wind. Actually Joe was havin' a pretty decent night's sleep, one of his rare ones and I wasn't about to wake him anyway, that's how faint some of the sounds were. But after a while I wasn't so sure it was just the wind and I did get up and go to the window to make certain. And that's when they came tear-assin' out. Didn't even have his headlights on either. I woke Joe then and we called the police. It wasn't till daylight that we saw the extent of the damage and we couldn't believe the wind masked all the noise the way it did. I told the police everything. First the young officer, Warren Blankfeld, and he was pretty impressed. Then Opie, and they both seemed as sure as I was who the culprit was. In fact Opie said he'd be closin' the case as soon as Seth showed up. Naturally when everybody got here the next mornin' I told them all what I knew too. Course, except for the Meshitskys. Better that the police handle that part. It must've taken hours to do the damage that they did. Every house on the bay looked like a maniac was on the loose. The glass sliders on each deck was shattered and inside things were broken and stuff missin' from every house. The Kosciusko place was one of the worst. Bottles of red wine were broken and it was all over the walls and white carpeting. They even threw one bottle through the TV screen. The Gorshins were missing a whole bunch of things. It took days to compile a list. The DiMarco house was ransacked, drawers pulled out and clothes ripped to shreds, particularly Mona's undergarments. Their espresso machine was fished out of the bay two days later and other things were never found. The Drake place was the worst of all. Almost everything was destroyed and the sick bastards urinated in their stove and refrigerator before they were done. Even the Meshitsky house wasn't spared, although it received the least damage. Mostly furniture overturned around the house and obscenities smeared on Lloyd and Shirley's bed linen with ketchup and mustard. Next to the bed, the police found a dead skunk wildly bobbing about, propelled by the powerful air jets of the giant whirlpool tub that dominated the otherwise sparse room. And much to Bunny's chagrin, every one of her bras and every pair of her panties were gone. Max Gorshin called a meetin' at his place that weekend and everybody was there, all except the Meshitskys as they weren't invited. Irene Drake was beside herself with fumin' anger, barely able to contain it. Her boys, a couple a years older than Seth, wanted to find him and beat him to a pulp. Marco too wanted to exact that brand of personal vengeance and not only on Seth and his pal but on Lloyd as well. Course, by then he had other reasons to want to break some of Lloyd's bones and he wasn't alone in that respect, everybody in the room havin' already been a victim of Lloyd's wrongdoin' to one degree or another. Mona, bein' a lawyer, said that kinda talk would just end em all in more trouble than the bastards themselves. Jacko and Spike were also voices of reason, in the end convincin' everyone to let the police handle the matter of the perpetrators and then lettin' the insurance companies, who were gonna be out a bundle, go after Lloyd. Joe chimed in sayin' whatever the law didn't take care of the Good Lord surely would. "Island justice" he called it, lookin' in my direction and knowin' I'd heard him use that expression once before. All that was needed was patience he was sayin', which I knew only too well that he himself had been demonstratin' for quite some time now. Well, as it turned out "Island justice," if there was such a thing, would have to do cause the law ended up doin' nothin' at all. And no amount of Opie's lame excuses about not havin' evidence did anything to dissuade us from what we all knew was the truth. He'd been paid off, plain and simple. And life on Bay Vista was never the same. That's "Never" with a capital N.

Eleven
The Big Screw

If there was any doubt on Lloyd's part that Seth was behind the mayhem that took place on Bay Vista it was erased as soon as he saw his bed sheets. *DIE. FUCKPRICK. SCUM. CPX. BAST.* Amidst the wild, abstract ketchup scrawls and crusted yellow mustard blotches those five distinct letter-assemblages were able to be discerned by anyone taking the time to look hard enough. Hearing from Detective Opelenczcic that a car resembling Seth's was seen fleeing the scene was superfluous as far as Lloyd was concerned. As was the fact that the detective was anxious to compare fingerprints taken from all the homes to those of Seth and his friend Butchie. The bed sheets were enough evidence for Lloyd. What to do about it was the question at hand.

He couldn't care less about what would happen to Seth if he were accused and convicted of the deed. But it would be disastrous to Lloyd. He was still two or three years away from his carefully planned departure and this would definitely upset the apple cart. It could very well ruin everything. He had to buy time. Not doing so would create too many problems to deal with at one time to be able to control. He'd be forced to speed up his *D-day* and that would be too costly, considering that scams promising to bolster his off-shore booty significantly were due to be completed in the near future.

The fact that his neighbors were beginning to bother him more and more on a regular basis about his dealings with them didn't cause him too much concern. He'd been able to hold them off so far and he was pretty sure he'd be able to continue long enough to escape relatively unscathed. In hindsight, he probably should have waited a little longer to start *shitting where he ate,* as the saying goes, but it was too late to do anything about that now. Stringing them along individually was a piece of cake but if they got together and found out he'd made patsies of *all* of them it might be a lot harder to handle. Especially without moving away from Bay Vista which he definitely did not want to do at this point. He was too close to his dream for a major upheaval like that to take place and interfere with his final preparations. There was just too much at stake.

It didn't matter to him either if people *thought* Seth was responsible for the vandalism. Thinking it, or even *knowing* it, was one thing. Proving it was quite another. It might add to the growing discomfort that Shirley, and possibly Bunny too, were already beginning to feel about the neighbors but that couldn't be avoided. Not at this point. He'd fed them stories many times before explaining away people's seeming hostility toward them and he'd have no trouble doing it again. And as distasteful as it might be, a truce of sorts would also have to be reached with Seth. At least for the time being. The only thing that really mattered was getting to D-day. Buying time was the only answer and, by far, the cheapest way to go. *Buying* being the operative word, Lloyd dialed Detective Opie's number and said he needed to meet with him privately.

* * *

That summer season, and the one that followed it, were

unlike any that went before on Bay Vista. Most, if not all, of the spontaneous fun that was such a part of everyday life seemed to be a thing of the past. An uneasiness settled in that was pervasive. After a time the residents became resigned to the fact that the violation to their homes and properties would go unpunished. The sight of Seth and his friend Butchie made them seethe on a daily basis. It was no secret that everyone believed they were guilty beyond any doubt and the two of them seemed to gloat about it. As far as everybody was concerned Lloyd was just as guilty as they were. The fix was in and everyone knew it. That was the only reasonable explanation for the case being dropped the way it had been. The ambivalence toward the Meshitsky women, evident during that first season following the incident, increasingly turned to intolerance by the second year. The vandalism, coupled with the facts of Lloyd having screwed everyone on the block slowly starting to leak out, served to isolate the Meshitskys. True to form, the *"them against us"* mindset kicked in and they continued their lives, still the center of attention. Only now they were alone on their prop-cluttered stage, playing to a silent, hostile audience. All but ostracized by those around them. If it bothered them at all they hardly showed it and, as a unit, they just circled the wagons and receded into a private bubble of an existence, defiantly giving a metaphorical finger to everyone on the outside.

* * *

Lloyd began devising the master plan that would govern the rest of his life as soon as he realized he'd have Shirley's inheritance to get him started. At some point early-on he dubbed his career endeavor *"The Big Screw."* As it progressed with more success than he could have imagined at first, he realized his original goal of becoming a "millionaire" was petty, considering he already had almost that much stashed away outside the country. And he'd been at it only two years. He also realized he didn't have a plan to speak of beyond achieving that threshold. That's when he dreamed up the "*D-day*" scenario. And that's when he realized a million dollars wouldn't be nearly enough to "drop out." At least not in the manner and style he'd like to. So he decided he needed a lot more. He set a new objective of ten million. The "big screw" would have to be really big. No longer could he be content with scamming clients, businesses, banks, and cheating strangers. They would continue to be his primary source of ever-replenishing patsies but in order to speed up the process he decided to include everyone along the way, meaning friends, a few of Shirley's relatives and neighbors too. But to keep everyday life from becoming too miserable and to stay one step ahead of the wrath of this group, the timing of the actual larceny would, by necessity, be much more critical.

He made an art form of deciding exactly how and when to bring people into "*the big screw.*" Some, like Joe Cooper, he determined didn't really matter. He was the first in Bayberry to fall victim to Lloyd and one of the few anywhere to have done so by sheer luck. Bad luck for Joe, good luck for Lloyd who, if not for a timely craving for a cold beer, would never have walked into the Jolly Roger tavern and bellied up to the bar next to a besotted Ben Bolen. Joe's contribution to Lloyd's D-day fund was worth $200,000. By extension, Drew Wicker and Atlantic Bank, being a part of the same scheme, added another $100,000 to the party, as Lloyd never made a single mortgage payment on the absurd loan he wangled. Drew was ultimately left to painstakingly cook the books in order to make the matter disappear. That was far preferable than trying to explain it.

Lloyd became a little overzealous though, miscalculating his drop-out timing by a good year and a half and started scamming his Bay Vista neighbors earlier than he should have. The first was Marco, who inadvertently added to Lloyd's illicit booty. Finally succumbing to Lloyd's constant pleading, and against his better judgment, he introduced him to one of his long time packaged-goods clients whose president was fascinated with what a marketing effort using the emerging sport of power boat racing might do for his products. The client swallowed Lloyd's spiel hook, line and sinker, and agreed to sponsor his make-believe racing team. That was almost two years before Lloyd actually started thinking seriously about a foray into the sport. By the time the client found out that Lloyd's entire pitch was trumped up and didn't own the boat he pretended to have, nor did he have an ounce of the experience he professed to possess, he had already made three $50,000 payments toward a promised $350,000 sponsorship deal. The client sued of course, but to no avail and ended up pulling his entire account from Marco's ad agency.

Doctors Max Gorshin and Rich Drake simply fell victim to Lloyd's earliest form of thievery and fraud, investing $20,000 each in one of his service stations. The money, along with that of a few others in the same deal, found its way into an off-shore bank account within six months.

Swifty Pearlstein made the mistake of taking on an impossible-to-win defense of one of Lloyd's shell companies in a case brought against it in northern New Jersey, losing over $16,000 in uncollected legal fees and disbursements.

Jacko was left holding the bag on the replacement cost of a forty-foot section of bulkhead on his and Lloyd's property that had sprung leaks, causing sink holes to form. Jacko laid out the full $11,000 cost, which was supposed to be split equally by both of them and never recouped a cent of Lloyd's share.

Lloyd convinced Harry Elias to establish a leasing subsidiary within his Chevy dealership rather than going through normal bank channels and charged him handsomely to help set it up. He then proceeded to lease two cars, one for Shirley and one for Bunny who hadn't even gotten a learner's permit yet, and failed to make a single payment on either one for almost two years. Harry, like the others, grudgingly endured Lloyd's inexhaustible stream of excuses and stalling tactics, too embarrassed to take any action.

The Mullins were lucky enough to escape his treachery, but only because they weren't all that friendly with the Meshitskys and Lloyd simply hadn't gotten around to figuring a way of fleecing them yet. Their business, a rather obscure one, just didn't offer Lloyd much opportunity to scam them. Mullin produced a certain type of wax that paper companies used to adhere the ends of paper towels and toilet paper to their cardboard tubes. And as diabolical a schemer as Lloyd was, this one stymied him.

The Bay Vista victims were only the tip of the iceberg, accounting for a relatively small percentage of Lloyd's hidden loot. But every little bit helped as Lloyd viewed it and somehow every one of these close-to-home scams seemed to provide him with far more personal fulfillment than most of the others. They were more of a challenge and being able to get away with it all was immensely satisfying. "*Nothing like fucking a friend*" he often mused, looking that person right in the eye, grinning as if nothing was awry and knowing the subject probably wouldn't even be raised, even after the victim was fairly certain he was being screwed over. Lloyd never ceased to be amazed that they all reacted in exactly the same manner. He could see it in their expressions, sense it in the halting way they spoke, their hoping that it would be Lloyd and not them who'd broach the subject. And Lloyd often did, feeding them one excuse or another, placating them with lies. And they all *wanted* to believe him. Believing him meant they weren't schmucks. Each proceeded through the various stages of whatever timeframe that particular person needed before finally arriving at the full, unavoidable recognition of having been given the shaft. Lloyd thought it funny that the wives always knew it first. And always showed it first.

J'net

Hard to believe is the only way to describe Opie's turnabout. All gung-ho one day, and the next, like it never even happened. Everybody was just madder'n hell and understandably so. A few came right out and practically accused him of bein' on the take. Right to his face. And Opie just fluffed it off like he didn't hear it. Max and Rich even went to the Mayor and complained but it never got em anywhere. I think Joe was upset more than anybody, sayin' Opie shamed himself. Aside from that he pretty much kept it inside, as was his nature. But that crime sure changed everything on Bay Vista. Probably just my imagination but I could swear there were more cloudy days and more rainy days that summer than ever before. Things somehow seemed gloomier and you could feel it in the air. At least I could, that's for certain. Joe Jr. came up for a few weeks that season. Which was real good for Joe and me cause it got our minds off the troubles somewhat. And that was when I first learned about the Meshitsky boy's gayness. Joe Jr. told me in no uncertain terms that it was a fact though he assured me he himself was not personally involved. But he said he knew someone who was which, to me, meant it probably was Father Kev, and that was the end of the discussion on the subject. I guess if anyone ever asked me who I most looked upon with enmity and bitterness in this world I would have to say it was Lloyd. Course, mainly for what he perpetrated on Joe, but even more so for him goin' out of his way to sorta rub it in his face, knowin' Joe couldn't do a thing about it. Like the time right after Joe Jr. left to go back to Belize that year and we were in the supermarket and along comes Lloyd and Shirley and he says to Joe, "Hey, neighbor, I saw that son of yours last week. Tell me something; is it true he's a faggot?" Well, Joe stopped dead in his tracks and, grippin' the handle of the shopping cart tighter'n hell, tried hard as he could to control himself while Lloyd and Shirley made their way toward the checkout, him laughin' like a damn hyena. I can say for a fact that that was the one and only time in my whole life when I completely lost my temper. And lost it good. I marched right up to Lloyd and squeezed in front of him in line and let loose with both barrels, givin' him a tongue-lashin' he wouldn't soon forget. And one that the crowd of people within earshot wouldn't either, so I'm told. Well, for the life of me I can't remember all that I said that day except that it ended with somethin' to the effect that, in case he didn't know it, his own son was a homosexual and maybe he should stop bein' so narrow-minded and show some tolerance and so forth and so on. I don't know just how long my tirade lasted or how loud it was but one thing's for sure: Lloyd was put in his place like never before. The color all but drained from his face and his upper lip was tremblin' and he stood there stone still while I let him have it and when I was finally finished there wasn't so much as a peep from him. I'm not too sure what was more devistatin' to Lloyd . . . the fact that his son was gay or that people might know about it. Judgin' by the way he was nervously eyin' everybody around him I'd probably have to go with the latter. As for Shirley, she never looked more perplexed than she did at that moment. I don't know whether Lloyd knew about Seth or not but I'd bet my bottom dollar that Shirley didn't. Of that I'm certain. Right about then Joe walked up and touched my arm. He was lookin' at me a little astounded at what I'd done cause he'd never seen me do anything like that before. Course, nobody else ever did either includin' myself, but I have to admit it sure felt exhilaratin' when it was over. Joe was pleased too, I could tell. And proud as could be. We left them standin' there and walked off to finish our shoppin' and this time it was us that couldn't keep from laughin' about it after a few minutes. I suppose that I was feelin' about the same as everybody else was around that time when it came to the Meshitskys. Like we all had about enough of em. Sorta like the vandalism was the straw that broke the camel's back. Funny how people put up with things until somethin' happens that makes what once could be overlooked no longer bearable. Like Lloyd cleanin' the damn engines on his damn boat. He'd hook up a garden hose to the engines one at a time and run water through em for a good fifteen or twenty minutes each. And more times than not he always did it around the dinner hour when everybody was tryin' to enjoy a peaceful meal. Damn engines would thunder nonstop for an hour so loud you couldn't even think straight. But people put up with it for years without sayin' too much. And mind you, those were years that they were still on speakin' terms with Lloyd. I can sorta understand it though. Like with Seth and his cacklin' drivin' people batty and nobody complainin' too vociferously about it until after he did his dirty deed. That's when people started lettin' their true feelin's make themselves known. No point in goin' to great lengths at tryin' to keep the peace any longer I guess. So every time Lloyd started cleanin' his engines I'd see one person or another come out on their deck and start yellin' at him. Usually one of the women. It was a little comical though cause nobody could hear a word that was bein' said over the noise of the motors roarin' like they were. Sorta like watchin' TV with the mute button on. Lips movin' but all you could ever hear was those damn engines. That damn boat of his made more noise than ten normal boats put together. Twenty maybe. One good thing though, seems that Seth's boat was no longer around to add to the din, and we were all thankful for that small favor. "Wild Cat" I believe he'd named it last year. Fitting, I suppose given who the owner was. Lloyd's new boat was named "CPA EXPRESS" just like his previous boats. Boring and pretty pretentious if you ask me. But that was Lloyd. Boring and pretentious. The other folks all had clever names on their boats. Marco named his after himself, his wife and his daughter, with a little dash of Eye-talian flavor thrown in, callin' it "PAPAMAMAMIA." Jacko's always made me laugh. "JUST VISITING" it said across its stern cause Jacko wanted everyone to believe he was some sort of space alien. What a pip! My favorites though were the two doctors' boats. They both played off their medical specialty and one was as witty as the other if you ask me. Rich named his "LADY FINGERS." Not one to be outdone by his partner, Max named his "INTERNAL AFFAIRS." I really got a kick out of those names. Still do. Joe though always blushed when somebody would mention em. Just like he would with off-color jokes. I guess that was the Quaker in him and in this day and age I suppose he was sorta funny that way. And people would sure let him know about it, good-naturedly of course. Which would only make him blush all the more. Anyway, the climate did really change after the break-ins happened and the most obvious, most glarin' difference was at the big season-endin' block party that summer. That difference bein' the Meshitskys weren't there. Not that anybody actually told em they weren't welcome. They were smart enough to figure that out for themselves. They made sure they were noticed though. Seth with his pain-in-the-ass cacklin' and Lloyd with his louder-than-hell boat runnin' this way and that all around the cove till the sun was down. But we were all happy they weren't amongst us. That's "Happy" with a capital H.

Twelve

I'm Spending!

The fact that his family never said a word about the tirade he went into at the dinner table when Lloyd coldly informed him that his boat was gone wasn't at all surprising to Seth. He'd gotten away with worse over the years. What *was* a surprise was that he and Butchie had somehow beaten the break-in rap when it looked like they were all but doomed. And it was surprising too that, so far, his father had let him off so easy. But he didn't for a moment expect it to last. Especially with Lloyd's knowing, apparently along with everybody else, that he and his friend were responsible for trashing all the houses. Including their own. It was the calm before the storm. He knew it. He fully expected to be the recipient of the worst consequences imaginable for causing what the entire neighborhood was now in a frenzy over. The prospect of jail had him poised to bolt the minute the situation got too hot. He and Butchie had already made plans to flee, probably to California, if they had to. It was definitely the first time that he actually regretted something he'd done, so terrified was he that maybe he'd finally gone too far.

When no charges materialized from the authorities, and when it didn't appear that they would, he could hardly believe it and felt enormously relieved to have at least dodged that bullet. Now he just needed to weather whatever rage would be coming from Lloyd. Making him sweat his fate for over a week, his father finally decided it was time to break his silence. He woke him at six A.M. one morning and made him walk down to the beach with him. Seth's trepidation grew with every step of the three-block trek. Although Lloyd had never once laid a hand on him, except for that one bloody nose, he was more than three times his size and easily could have beaten him into oblivion any time he wanted to. Arriving at the deserted, dreary beach that morning, that's exactly what Seth was expecting.

The sky was overcast and a thick, wet fog was fast approaching over the ocean. It consumed the pounding surf like a soft, porous whitewashed wall and continued onto the beach and finally engulfed them both, making everything except the two of them totally disappear. The air was dank with its moving moisture and Seth could feel the goose bumps forming as he gripped his arms in an attempt to ward off the shivers that had taken hold of his body. Was he cold or afraid, he asked himself. *Both*, he thought, trying to decide if he should make a run for it before the blows, which he was certain were about to begin, would start raining down on him. But none were forthcoming. Only words.

"I've made a decision."

Lloyd was staring ahead, seeing not a thing through the dense soup that completely obliterated anything beyond a few feet from where they stood. Seth was glad that his father preferred staring at nothingness rather than at him at that moment. Much safer, he reasoned and joined in, thinking this is what it must feel like to be blind. Staring at white nothingness, day in and day out. Pretty cool, in a strange sort of way.

"I've decided that selling your boat is enough punishment for you. At least for the time being."

Seth stood silently, *blindly* gazing straight ahead, the

fear he felt minutes earlier starting to disappear, as if sucked into the all-claiming fog along with his father's words.

"What you did was nearly disastrous to my plans. You know what plans I'm talking about. It cost me dearly to make things right again and your stupid stunt is going to make things very unpleasant around here for the next two years. Two years. That's what I'm looking at. Thanks to you things are going to be extremely hairy now for the duration and I can't afford any more crap from you. Am I making myself clear?"

Seth was afraid to say a word. What he was hearing gave him hope that the worst may have been over. His father was talking to him again. And about D-day too, of all things. This wasn't turning out to be as bad as he thought it would.

"I expect you to toe the line. Two years. One more fuck-up and all bets are off. I'll turn you over to the cops faster than you can say '*fruitcake*' and they can throw away the fucking key for all I care. Is that understood?"

Seth nodded and said "Yes." His relief mixing with elation in ways he thought he forgot how to feel, he turned to look at Lloyd who was still staring into the fog. Fearing he hadn't heard his answer he said it again, louder. "Yes."

Lloyd turned and without another word started walking away and, though Seth didn't know it, he was leaving his son to fend for himself, literally and figuratively, for the rest of his life. Lloyd had made another decision, one that he didn't let on that morning. Seth was no longer a part of the D-day adventure.

Seth watched him go, disappearing after taking only a dozen steps as if he was never even there. He stayed there on the beach for almost an hour, hearing the surf and looking into the whiteness that enveloped him. Blind as a bat and happy as a pig in shit.

* * *

For the first time in almost seven years Seth was without a boat of his own for the summer. Gone with it was his status, real or imagined, as a big shot in the eyes of everyone he knew. Even Butchie started coming around less than he did before. Taking turns on Seth's Jet Ski was a far cry from tooling around the bay in a powerful boat and nowhere as impressive to others in their age group. Besides, Seth's agonizing, newly forced good citizenship meant that most of their black-hearted behavior had to be kept under wraps and that just wasn't as much fun. The delight in seeing the effects that some of their dastardly antics had on people was, by necessity, limited to those times when Lloyd wasn't around, which were few and far between.

Butchie wasn't the water sports type and when he was there they spent much of their time just idly hanging around the house and its property, making snide remarks about anyone who might be about, then laughing their heads off as loud as they could at whatever it was. They knew that just the sight of the two of them, especially if they were having fun, pissed the neighbors off no end, and they made sport of letting them know that they knew it.

They were down near the bulkhead one day, just catching some rays and shooting the breeze. Bored stiff. A light fog started rolling in around them and they felt the sudden chill that always accompanies fog but it wasn't cold enough to interrupt their lazing.

"Hey, Butchie, did you ever wonder what it feels like being blind?"

"I got better things to think about."

"Yeah, like what?"

"Like your sister's tits."

"I'm serious. Close your eyes. Tell me what you see."

"I see your sister's tits. And her ass. And her . . ."

Seth threw a pebble at him, saying "No, be serious for one fucking minute. Do you think if you're blind you see just blackness or just whiteness?"

"How the fuck should I know? Maybe they see big black and white tits!" Butchie said, his lowbrow wit sending him into convulsive laughter.

"I'm thinking whiteness," Seth continued. "I bet it's pretty cool in a way. Being blind I mean."

"You're fucking nuts. White, black, what difference does it make? Either way it's gotta suck."

"A laser can blind you."

"What?"

"You know, a laser beam. If it's powerful enough it can blind you."

"No shit?"

"It's common knowledge."

"Not that common. I never knew it."

"How the fuck could you? You can't read worth a shit. They got TV in that hellhole swamp where you live?"

"There's TV there."

"Then you should watch it. Maybe you'd learn something."

"Fuck you. And your sister." Butchie paused for effect and winked at Seth before continuing. "How about I fuck you *and* your sister?" which sent him into another fit of laughter. He laughed so hard and so long that, when it looked as if he'd never stop, Seth couldn't keep from joining in.

After a while the fog drifted away as fast as it had arrived and they both sat there, pensively watching tiny sparkles of reflected sunlight flickering off the bay's low carpet of ripples.

"Maybe we should get one. You know, a laser," Butchie said.

"Yeah. That's what I was thinking."

* * *

On days when Butchie wasn't around, Seth split his time either speeding around the bay on his Jet Ski or at the beach. On days when the surf was up, he'd usually be at the beach from dawn to dusk with his board. Rainy days, of which there seemed to be too many recently, would find him at Saint Josephat's. Not for anything having to do with piety, faith or reverence, but to hone his swimming and diving skills at the huge indoor pool complex. That, along with some other things that developed over time. He'd started going there over a year ago and in the beginning had kept it a secret, not really wanting anyone to get the impression that he'd have anything to do with church. *After all,* he liked thinking to himself, *I have a reputation to protect.* More recently he was keeping it a secret because of the other activities he began to indulge in. Activities that started toward the end of last year.

Father Kev was a frequent visitor to the sports complex and, having always been an avid swimmer himself, especially to the pool and its adjoining locker and shower facilities. Seth had seen him many times before because he never failed to come to the Bay Vista block parties, having always been invited by old man Cooper. Seth caught him watching him intently one day in the locker room and figured it was because he recognized *him* from the parties as well. The same thing happened on several other occasions. He'd look up and see him standing not far away. Seth was becoming increasingly aware that he was very definitely the object of the priest's furtive glances.

One day, when Seth was about to leave the locker room, he felt a hand on his shoulder and turned to find himself face to face with Father Kev.

"I'm Father Flaherty. Father Kev to most people. I couldn't help noticing you here the past few weeks. You're a superb swimmer."

Seth didn't say anything. He finished packing his gym bag and started to go.

"You're from Bay Vista aren't you?"

"Yeah," Seth answered.

"I knew it! Second house from the street, right?"

"Yeah, that's right."

"What's your name, if I may ask?"

"Seth."

"Seth, that's right. I think I remember hearing that. At one of the block parties. How old are you, Seth? Eighteen? Nineteen?"

"Nah. I won't even be seventeen for another three months."

"Really! Could've fooled me," the priest said, smiling and adding, "Pretty big and strong-looking for just sixteen."

Seth didn't mind hearing that. He wanted to look older.

"You know, Seth, there's something I'd like to share with you. I think you'll be happy to hear it too. Come, walk with me, won't you?"

Father Kev took Seth's arm and led him out of the sports facility and across the parking lot, giving him a history of his time at Saint Josephat's, beginning with his being an altar boy. As they walked toward the church and its adjoining rectory the priest went on and on about how, over the years, the building had been transformed from the once-tiny original into the modern, impressive structure that it was today. Seth, who was bored out of his mind, nevertheless continued listening, worried that if he was his usual rude self it might end up costing him his pool privileges. They were nearing the side door of the church building and Seth, having no real desire to go in, finally decided he just couldn't take any more. He stopped and, as out-of-character as it was for him, politely said, "Look Father, I think maybe you were wrong. I'm not really too interested in all this stuff. So maybe I should just . . ."

Father Kev held up a hand, stopping him in mid-sentence. "Seth, this isn't what I wanted to speak to you about. Please," he said, taking his arm again. "Come with me."

They entered the church. Seth was shocked at the sheer size of the space. And at the surprisingly different atmosphere the interior architecture portrayed from that of the exterior. Outside was all modern in its design as well as in the contemporary materials used in its construction. A mixture of steel and glass—both mirrored and stained—massive vertical stucco panels set into wide, blonde, lacquered hardwood columns, and two stylized interpretations of a crucifix atop tapered spires that flanked the bell tower. Inside though, was like stepping back in time. Dark, ornate, a domed ceiling not even visible from the outside, carved balustrades with stone coping supporting a wraparound balcony, vividly painted statues everywhere and a cathedral-like, gilded multi-level altar spanning the entire width of the cavernous room.

Father Kev led Seth across the front of the church, between the altar and the first row of pews, stopping briefly in the center aisle to genuflect, and then continued on through another door on the opposite side. They walked along a low-ceilinged hallway past many closed doors, making several turns and finally arriving at the rectory area. Father Kev's living quarters. They were in an anteroom outside his office. He opened the door and motioned to Seth to follow.

"Have a seat, Seth." The priest walked to a high-backed leather chair and sat, watching Seth take in the whole scene. He remembered the first time he saw this room himself. It hardly changed at all since he was a boy, and he remembered too how impressive and imposing it was then.

Seth sat on the couch, upholstered in the same dark, wine-colored leather as the rest of the room's furnishings and looked at the priest who, in an effort to put Seth at ease, tried to strike as relaxed a pose as he could. He propped both feet on the edge of the coffee table that separated them, raised an index finger to his lips and closed his eyes for a few moments before speaking.

"Seth, as I said before, I've noticed you on several occasions here at Saint Josephat's and, though we've never talked, I believe I know a great deal about you."

Seth said nothing. He put his feet up on the corner of the table, mimicking the priest and stared silently across at him.

"I believe I know you because I believe we have a lot in common. When I said you were a superb swimmer I meant it. But I'm sure you know that. Actually you remind me of myself when I was your age. Younger in fact. I think I was only fourteen or fifteen when I first used the pool here."

Not a reaction of any kind from Seth.

"Actually, swimming isn't the only similarity I've noticed and of course that's not the reason I wanted to speak with you. Seth, I want you to know that you shouldn't be ashamed about the things you're feeling."

Seth's stare was icy cold.

"I think you know what I'm talking about. Am I right? Seth, am I right?"

Nothing from Seth. Not so much as a blink of his eyes.

"I once had much the same reaction as I've seen in you. You know what I'm talking about don't you? I'm talking about the shower room, Seth. I've been there myself. Long, long ago. It's okay. I understand and I'm here for you. I want you to know that."

Father Kev watched Seth for some sort of reaction. And when it finally came he didn't know what to make of it. He thought he saw Seth smile, but maybe it was a sneer. He couldn't be sure. And then he made the oddest sound.

"*AAHK!*"

* * *

Each time Joe Jr. came back to the Reach he did so with mixed emotions. At first his lifestyle was something he was never comfortable with around family. By the time that didn't seem to be as much of a problem to him as it was before, he'd met his *partner* Joe. After hooking up with him, the possibility of coming back to the Island permanently was put on indefinite hold. Their jobs were in Belize and, though he could always find a bank to work for fairly easily, the same wasn't true for Joe. His graphic design business was finally doing okay. He'd invested too much time developing his client base to be able to just pick up and go. It would take years to build it up again in a new locale and that would mean years of making little or no money. But each time Joe Jr. visited he realized he really missed the place. He missed being a part of his father's life. Especially now that he had J'net who he absolutely adored. In fact, it didn't take Joe Jr. very long to realize that *he* absolutely adored her too. She had that effect on most people.

No visit to the Reach would be complete without spending a good deal of time with Kev. They were such close pals for so long that they were like long-lost brothers each time they saw one another these days.

His trip up this time around though wasn't a planned

one and he never let Kev know in advance that he was coming. The main reason was because he sensed that his father and J'net were a little shaken by what transpired across the way at Bay Vista and they sounded like they could use a visit from him. And fast. Crime like that wasn't something they were used to. Nobody on the Reach was used to it.

It was a couple of days before he got around to calling Kev and, after he did, they got together often during the remainder of his visit. He was driving by Saint Josephat's one day when he realized that he'd forgotten to invite Kev to dinner that night even though J'net had reminded him to do so more than once. He swung the car into the parking lot and headed straight for the rectory thinking, at this late in the day, that's probably where he'd find him.

Joe Jr. wasn't a Catholic but he knew Saint Josephat's better than most people who were. He spent time here when he was a kid and Kev was an altar boy. And after Kev became its pastor Saint Josephat's was like a second home whenever Joe Jr. visited. Cognacs and cigars in Kev's study and reminiscing old times had become a ritual they both cherished and one that was absolutely mandatory, usually more than once on each one of his trips north.

He made his way through the maze of hallways that were a part of the original building and reached the anteroom of Kev's apartment. He walked to the door of his office and was about to knock when the sound he heard stopped him dead in his tracks. It was a sound he'd heard before. And a sound he'd heard *of* many times before as well. He waited, hoping he was wrong, but he heard it again.

"*AAHK, AAHK.*"

Then he heard what he was hoping he wouldn't. Kev's unmistakable voice. But saying what? He couldn't tell. Then the other person again.

"*AAHK, AAHK, AAHK, AAHK.*"

Then Kev again.
"Seth!"
"*AAHK.*"
"Seth!"
"*AAHK, AAHK.*"
"Seth, I'm going to *spend!*"
"*AAHK.*"
"Spend with me, Seth! Spend with me!"
"*AAHK, AAHK, AAHK.*"
"Oh God, I'm *spending.* I'm *SPENDING!!!*"
"*AAHK.*"

Joe Jr. went over to a chair against the far wall and sat there, waiting. He waited about ten minutes and the door finally opened. Seth walked out and saw him sitting there and strode right on by, staring him straight in the eye as he passed, half smiling, half sneering. But underneath that façade was unmistakable fear. Fear that now everyone would know. Kev came out a minute later and sat next to him, trying as hard as he could not to make eye contact.

"Jesusfuckingchrist, Kev!"
"Joe, please. Stop."
"He's just a *kid,* Kev!"
"He's older than we were, Joe."
"Jesusfuckingchrist!"
"Joe, please don't say that" Kev said, just like he did decades ago, only this time adding, "You're in a house of God."

Joe Jr. slapped himself on the forehead and thought *Jesusfuckingchrist!*

J'net

Number three surely had the most numbing effect on me. They say time heals all wounds and I suppose it's true cause the first two didn't seem to be half as tragic as this one. Course, at the time maybe they were. Hard for me to remember, though. But this one somehow was the most painful. Even though I did feel sorta numb throughout the whole ordeal. Numb to everything except the pain of havin' the most special person you ever knew snatched away and suddenly bein' all alone again. Such true heartache. Maybe losin' your mate at this stage in life makes you realize how close you are to followin' along right behind him. Which I'm sorta ready for. Anyway, to hear some people talk, it was the biggest funeral the Reach ever saw. I guess in all those years Joe touched a lot of lives and touched em in ways that made a difference cause there were people I never even knew existed that came to pay their respects. Too many to count. Roland and Drew and Bonnie tried explainin' who was who but I couldn't follow a lot of what was goin' on. Numbness and pain. Pain and numbness. And the line between em so thin you can't even tell em apart most of the time. Everybody from Bay Vista was there even though it was still off-season and all the houses were still closed up. Course, no Meshitskys thank heavens! But everyone wanted to know what they could do, especially Mona. But there wasn't much anybody could do except bein' there like they were. Afterwards, Joe Jr. and Joe stayed with me for a good month before havin' to go back to Belize and I don't know what I would've done without em durin' those days. After they left it was still several weeks before the season would be in swing again and I guess that was the loneliest time of all. The neighborhood was empty. The house was empty. My life was empty. The Reach without Joe Cooper just wasn't right. Not for me, that's for certain. I guess that's when I started thinkin' about maybe leavin' and goin' down to Belize. Maybe in the fall. Dependin' on how the summer went. Course, the summer got under way right on schedule on Memorial Day weekend. And the damn Meshitskys were there earlier, just like always. Not one word of condolences from any of em either. Which was just fine with me. When everybody else started arrivin' though, I was kept pretty busy. Everybody goin' out of their way and doin' whatever they could to make sure I was okay.

There wasn't a week that went by without someone invitin' me over for dinner. More than once. And when they went out to their Eye-talian place they'd always try draggin' me with em too. Sometimes wouldn't take no for an answer. Marco even came over to have a scotch with me on several occasions which was real sweet of him. Course, there was many a night when I'd just as soon like to be alone. I'd have my evenin' scotch and watch the sunset and remember how special these last twelve years were. And I'd talk to Joe. Not out loud, just to myself. But I know he was hearin' me. Last summer was sorta odd because of the break-ins and all. Things changed and it felt different. So much tension in the air. Maybe that's why Joe left us when he did. He didn't like what was happenin' on his beloved Reach. Well, at least his passin' was peaceful and painless. Except for the unrest and pain that I know he had in his heart because of all the trouble across the way in Bay Vista. Anyway, I'd sip my scotch, alone with my thoughts of Joe and I'd tell him that maybe things would get better. What I didn't know yet though, and what I couldn't tell him was this: Not before they got worse. That's "Worse" with a capital W. And it sure took its sweet time arrivin' too. Maybe because we all sorta expected somethin' bad was on its way. Not like last year wasn't bad enough what with all the vandalism and all. And then my losin' Joe on top of everything else. The whole summer seemed to just drag on and on. To me, at least. In slow motion, goin' toward somethin' you maybe didn't want to see but goin' there just the same.

Thirteen
Not without a Mirror

Every year the permanent population on the Reach increased a little. More and more of the visitors, mostly the summer residents, decided that's where they wanted to spend their retirement years. In contrast to the bustling vitality that was the Island during the summer months, the off-season was a picture of perfect tranquility. Most of the businesses closed, many right after Labor Day and others for just three or four months during the dead of winter. Some whose goods and services were more of an essential nature stayed open all year long for the growing number of families that remained on the Island, even though they were likely losing money every day.

It was bitter cold much of the time with a relentless west wind coming off the bay. Lying five miles off the mainland like a giant sandbar, the Reach rarely received any significant snow so travel was hardly ever a problem, especially with so few cars on the road. The traffic lights were all put on blinker mode and the speed limit was increased by ten miles per hour.

The colors of the sky and the water were a little less vivid but the sunrises and sunsets were still spectacular and if bundling up in layers for a brisk, invigorating walk on a desolate beach with no one to talk to but seagulls and sandpipers was your thing, then this was the place to be. Peace and quiet was the order of the day, every day. Weeks could go by when the most exciting thing to happen might be the daily arrival of mail. So, in its own unique way, for those who liked it, the Reach was just as pleasurable a paradise in the winter as it was in the summer.

Over the years, both the DiMarcos and the Kosciuskos had given more and more thought to one day joining the growing ranks of those that called the Reach their permanent home. Those ranks were due to increase significantly in the not-too-distant future when the leading wave of baby boomers, of which Marco and Jacko were members, would begin reaching retirement age. Lately, though, both families harbored some uneasiness about that prospect. Sandwiched between their two houses were the Meshitskys and the climate on Bay Vista was definitely in flux over recent events, giving pause to some of their thinking. In each of their cases a decision was still a decade away but doubts and uncertainty were now mixed in with what had always been almost a foregone conclusion in their minds. There was only one thing that could happen that would alleviate the concerns they were having: The swine next door had to go.

* * *

The summer following the vandalism, and the next one too, were markedly different in that the residents of Bay Vista were no longer able to just look the other way and ignore things the way they had in the past. The lack of any progress on the part of the police to bring the case to a conclusion made peoples' blood boil. And this was exacerbated each time they'd see or hear Seth do or say something that pissed them off. And it wouldn't take much. Just the sight of him, especially if he was with his friend and partner in crime, was usually enough to make them fume.

Shirley and Bunny were increasingly keeping out of sight, staying indoors most of the time, even on beautiful days. On occasions when they did venture outdoors they would brazenly glare at their neighbors as if what had happened was all their fault. Conversation between the Meshitskys and everyone else was a thing of the past.

If there was one thing that infuriated everyone, one thing that provoked their wrath more than anything else, it was probably when Lloyd cleaned the engines on his boat. It was an act that somehow became symbolic of the disdain that Lloyd and, by extension, his family had for their neighbors. The noise was excruciatingly loud and experiencing it almost every evening had become unbearable to everyone except the Meshitskys themselves, who would sit on their deck and pretend not to hear the neighbors' screaming complaints. In reality it was fairly impossible to hear anything over the deafening thunder of the engines but Lloyd also pretended not to see them. Mostly it was the women who emerged onto their decks and lost their tempers.

Had there been a lip-reader present to witness the scenes he would have gotten an eyeful of extraordinarily colorful and expressive language from the ladies of Bay Vista.

Carrie Gorshin: *"YOUR MOTHER SHOULD'VE HAD AN ABORTION YOU FUCKING ASSHOLE DICKHEAD PRICK!"*

Spike Kosciusko: *"BLOW IT OUTA YOUR ASS YOU FAT SCUMBAG PIG!"*

Irene Drake: *"YOUR PECKER SHOULD TURN BLACK AND FALL OFF IN YOUR HAND YOU POLISH PIECE OF SHIT!"*

Mona DiMarco: *"EAT SHIT AND DIE, LLOYD. THEN ROT IN HELL!"*

Lloyd and his family were oblivious to it all. Or pretended to be.

*   *   *

There were three schools of thought about what, if anything, should be done about the situation on Bay Vista. And as far as the residents were concerned the lines that delineated the three weren't hard and fast. While each person may have favored one "*option*" as they were called, over the other two, there was certain wisdom along with varying degrees of appreciation in all three of them among each individual.

The topic never failed to come up when they were together as a group, most often when out to dinner at *La Sabbia*, the restaurant that became an instant hit the day it was opened by the brothers Altadonna, re-transplanted back to their native New Jersey after their successful stint in Napa Valley.

The Bay Vista group was the restaurant's best customers from the very beginning and had a standing Saturday night reservation at a special table of their own, which was set off all by itself in a semi-private alcove near the kitchen. The spot was good for two reasons and both Valdo and Enzo laid claim to having had the original idea of seating them there. Valdo, in charge of the dining room, knew from experience that the group was at times inclined toward being a tad boisterous before the evening was over and this bit of privacy was good for them as well as the other patrons. Enzo, the master and "*artiste*" of the kitchen, had a different but even more valid reason. The Meshitskys, at least in the beginning, were often a part of the group and he was convinced that the appalling sight of Lloyd was enough to make people lose their appetites. If not the contents of their stomachs! Further infuriating was the fact that "*Porco,*" as he was referred to by the entire staff, never failed to disrupt the kitchen by specially requesting an order of French fried potatoes which, to Enzo's continuing dismay, his brother always acquiesced to. And regardless of how many tubers the cooks dropped everything for to hurriedly peel, slice and fry, or how high the grease-laden platter was piled when it finally made its arrival at the table, it was always received with the same arrogant comment from the repugnant pig-man: "What am I, anemic?"

At Enzo's insistence, Lloyd was henceforth assigned the seat in the farthest corner of the alcove, out of sight from the rest of the dining room. And that's where he stayed until he and his wife abruptly stopped coming. The "*gang of ten,* as they eventually became affectionately known as, were the mainstay of the Saturday night alcove room and they included the Kosciuskos, DiMarcos, Gorshins, Drakes and Pearlsteins. They were often joined by others but, mercifully, never again by the Meshitskys.

* * *

They were almost finished with their appetizers, the remains of the hot antipasto, calamari salad and artichoke platters making their way around the table, the contents of each quickly disappearing at each stop. Spearing the last of the fried zucchini with his fork, Max was saying, "Why don't we just take a vote."

They were already through the first three of the ten outstanding bottles of wine they customarily consumed—five whites and five reds—and the conversation turned to what it inevitably always did, their now-despised neighbors. There were three distinct camps, each advocating a different course and, although each camp had its own primary advocate, their actual membership fluctuated wildly from week to week, allegiance shifting from one to another depending on just how pissed off a person might be at any given moment.

Max was all for taking the lawsuit route but, ironically, was usually discouraged by the two lawyers in the group, Mona and Swifty, who both argued that it wasn't worth the time and effort and even if they ended up winning they'd still end up losing. Carrie thought that that didn't even make sense, and of course she was right. But, then again, she wasn't. Daphne, at the moment, agreed with her best friend but also agreed with her husband and Mona, and was now leaning toward joining the Kosciusko camp, at least for tonight. Jacko was perhaps the biggest proponent of the "*Joe Cooper philosophy,*" which meant he preferred seeing how things played out while letting a higher power deal with them. Spike was usually in that camp too but, occasionally, this night being one of those occasions, she was more in the mood to side with Irene, who was the most steadfast among them in never veering from her position. She wanted to take the law into her own hands, campaigning non-stop for some sort of physical suffering to be inflicted on Seth and Lloyd both. Rich was torn between his partner's litigation viewpoint and his wife's vigilante approach. The instant personal gratification aspect of Irene's "*beat the shit out of them*" scenario was hard to ignore and usually swayed Rich in that direction. Marco pretty much always sided with Irene and, when he did, Mona would always elbow him in the ribs. Marco's rationale was that that was the way things were handled on the streets of the Bronx and that's where he grew up and, besides, that's probably the only thing those two would understand anyway. Which always got a few nods of agreement, but not always from the same people. Except for Irene, who always emphatically agreed, often going so far as to offer up some specific proposals on the damage that should be done.

"Arms are better than legs," she'd argue.

"How so?" Spike asked.

"Because if both their arms were in casts for two or three months, Shirley would have to wipe their asses."

"Good point," Rich had to admit.

"And when the casts came off we could break them again." Irene was serious.

Marco chimed in with, "You know, one phone call to my Uncle Carmine back in New York and it's a done deal."

Another elbow to the ribs from Mona.

And so it would go until someone changed the subject, which wasn't often.

Another exquisite meal was had by all and by the time the dishes were cleared from the table the restaurant was empty of that night's other customers and Valdo and Enzo had joined them, as was their custom, to help finish the two remaining bottles of wine. Espressos and cappuccinos were being served by "Mutt," the nickname given to one of the waiters who happened to be short; and *"Jeff,"* a waiter who went by that nickname because he was tall, was pouring Sambuca all around. Their real names were Sean and Doug respectively but that didn't matter. Everyone who worked at the restaurant was given a nickname on their first day on the job and that was the name that stuck with them whether they liked it or not.

The Altadonna brothers knew all about the problems at Bay Vista and they both commiserated with everyone about it. They also made no secret that they hated it back in the days when Lloyd would be in the place and they always made sport of deriding *"Porco"* every chance they could. Mutt and Jeff weren't exactly silent about their view of him either, due probably to the meager tip he would customarily leave.

The *gang of ten* always lingered long after closing time with Valdo and Enzo and the evening wouldn't end before the group's need to verbally drub away at the Meshitskys had been sated. It was a temporary addiction that they all had and getting a weekly fix of it would have to do until some permanent resolution could be reached.

That night's primary target happened to be Shirley and, Irene, who was in rare form, currently had the floor. After several minutes of general Shirley-bashing she settled into a riotous theme of what Shirley's sex life must be like with her "*blubberman*" that had the whole table in side-splitting stitches.

Mona stopped laughing long enough to interject, saying, "Wait . . . I have it straight from the horse's mouth that she hasn't slept with Lloyd in at least five years. At least not in the biblical sense!"

"Really? She actually told you that?"

"Yes, she most certainly did, maybe two years ago. Of course, at that time it had only been three years."

Irene cracked up, spurting out her words between fits of laughter, "Poor Shirley probably hasn't even seen Lloyd's pecker in five years!"

To which Swifty said, "I got news for you . . . poor Lloyd hasn't seen it in a lot longer than that. Not without a mirror."

And with that absurdly comical visual popping into everyone's mind, the table erupted again into wave after wave of totally uncontrollable laughter.

J'net

Cruelness is something I don't think I'll ever understand no matter how long I live. It's all around us all the time. You read about it and you see it on TV and usually when you hear about it you have to just shake your head cause it's always bein' done to the most innocent and least deservin' among us. It's one thing if somebody deserves it I suppose, like an eye for an eye sorta thing. But when you're cruel for no reason I just can't understand it. Like abusin' kids and even babies. If somebody hurts you it's natural to want to hurt em right back and that's human nature I guess. But a little kid? A defenseless baby? The sufferin' some of em are subjected to is just too sad to even think about. Or imagine. And the people who do these things aren't just sick. No, callin' em sick's too good for em. Evil. But that's even too good for em if you ask me. Cause the poor victim was never deservin' of the cruelty. Animals too. People are cruel to animals all the time and for the life of me it's somethin' I'll just never understand. Why do people get kicks outa stuff like that? I'm not talkin' about huntin'. Huntin's been around forever and it's been necessary. Course, these days that's not as true as it once was. Except in parts of the world where there's still a need for it for survival purposes. But cruelty is another matter all together. There's never been a reason for that and there never will. Evil. Maybe that's as close as you can get to describin' it after all. Like the evil little bastard over in Bay Vista. This year he's got himself a new toy. One of those new "laser" things that shoots some kinda ray of light. And it goes as far as it has to till somethin' in its path stops it. It'll probably go clear across the bay. Farther than that probably. At first he was just pointin' at things and makin' a red dot move around and people didn't know what was goin' on. But I heard somewhere that it's a dangerous thing to play with cause it can be harmful to the eyes. If the light hits you in the eye that is. Blind you even. And he must've heard the same thing cause recently him and his damn friend have taken to pointin' the thing at seagulls and I just know they're tryin' to hit em in the eyes. A seagull'd be sittin' on one of the dock pilings mindin' his own business and they'd be aimin' the ray or beam or whatever it's called at it and be movin' it around tryin' to make it stop in the unsuspectin' bird's eye. I can tell that's what they're doin' by the way they react when the gull flies away cause it's flyin' crazily like maybe it's hurt. And they're laughin' like there's no tomorrow. That's pure cruelty. And pure evil. Spike saw em one time and yelled at em to stop and I guess they did. But they were at it the very next day again and this time someone called the police cause Warren Blankfeld showed up and was talkin to them and to Lloyd for some time before he left. I wish he'd taken the laser thing away from them but he didn't. From then on I think Seth just continued doin' it on the sly cause there were plenty of occasions that we'd see seagulls flyin' around erratically. We just never saw where he was doin' it from. It had everyone a little on edge though cause there wasn't a person among us that didn't think he was just practicin' on the birds. Nobody would put it past him to turn the damn thing on people next. In fact we all expected it. We never talked about it in so many words but we were all thinkin' it. Trepidation day after day. But the summer went on at a snail's pace and it was finally the middle of August and the block party was just two weeks away and we'd gotten this far without him blindin' anybody. Or tryin' to. But that didn't put anybody at ease, that's for sure. Just the opposite. That's "Opposite" with a capital O.

Fourteen
Double Flipping of the Bird

People always looked forward to the Bay Vista block party with mixed emotions. It was definitely the highlight of the season when the most fun was had by everyone. But it also meant the end of the summer and a return to another too-long period of grey weather, toil and drudgery at work and school. This year though seemed different. No one actually talked about it but as the Labor Day weekend approached there was a sense of anxiety that everyone was harboring, as if they couldn't wait to finally have the season ended.

The normal big crowd was expected again for the Sunday bash and, on Saturday night, the "*gang of ten*" was assembled at La Sabbia for their traditional season-ending swan song dinner. It would be almost another nine months before they'd be doing it again and this last night out was always a special one. There were no holds barred when it came to wines that were selected on this night, and the same would be true for the following day. Most of the conversation was centered on what everyone was planning to cook for the party. Some people eat to live. This group lived to eat.

"Rich had an exceptional *yellow-fin* season this year," Irene was saying. "So we're doing a whole medley of tuna stuff."

"Mmm, like what?" Max asked.

"Well, first we're doing the usual whole smoked fish. That's always a good starter. Later we'll have Thai tuna burgers with ginger-lemon mayonnaise and then of course the grilled tuna steaks with garlic butter."

"I'm slow-roasting some pork tenderloins with a dijon mustard and orange marmalade marinade," Carrie offered. "And what, pray tell, will the Kosciuskos treat us to this year?"

"I'm still stuck in my poultry period," Spike said. "So I'm doing roasted capons with herb butter and porcini-madeira sauce. And I'm trying to talk Jacko into making his zuppa di pesce. It's my all-time personal favorite," she added with a wink in his direction. Jacko shook his head and blushed. "And I presume you're in charge of the salad again, Swifty?"

"Salads. With an 's'. Sweet onions, anchovies, capers, bean sprouts, seaweed, endive slaw and spicy Asian tofu-crusted cucumbers. That's one. And another with shaved asparagus, Mandarin oranges, beets, warm green bell peppers, pecorino, almonds and wilted watercress. And if I have time, maybe a smoky eggplant, fennel, Moroccan arugula, crispy shallots, cornbread croutons with a mushroom-infused, ricotta-syrah vinaigrette. Oh, and potato salad."

"That means he's making potato salad. *Only* potato salad," Daphne informed the table. "Okay Mona, you're on."

"Well, it's been a few years since I last made it and it was always such a big hit, especially with all the kids, so I was thinking of maybe just going back to my lasagna."

"Actually it's my mother's lasagna," Marco corrected her.

"No, actually it's my great aunt's lasagna," Mona corrected him back.

"My mother's," Marco assured the others again and, before Mona could answer, changed the subject to the possibility of someday retiring on the Reach. Jacko and Spike said they were leaning toward doing that too.

Irene shook her head, saying "It's a frigging ghost town here during the rest of the year. What the hell would you do with your time?"

"I don't know. Write a book, maybe. The great American novel!" Marco said.

"What about?"

"Us. All this," he answered, with a sweeping gesture of his arm.

There followed a spirited discussion of the actors who should play each of their characters in the movie adaptation and there were only two things they were all in agreement on: Spike would be portrayed by Sharon Stone; and no one was fat enough to faithfully portray Lloyd. The conversation deteriorated into wildly imaginative and somewhat macabre suggestions on how the story should end. None, however, as wild or macabre as what was actually about to transpire.

* * *

The weather usually cooperated for the residents of Bay Vista on the Sunday before Labor Day. In fact, only once since the block parties started was rain ever a problem and, even then, not a big one. The festivities were simply moved to the ample space under the Kosciusko and Gorshin houses where the revelry proceeded relatively unaffected, except for a few raindrops falling on people when they walked between those two protected areas.

This year's forecast was a glorious one weather-wise. The humidity was low, as was the wind and the sky was as clear as could be. Fall was just around the corner and, perhaps for the first time, that fact seemed to be a welcomed prospect for the Bay Vista people. A strangely perceptible uneasiness belied the picture-perfect calmness of the day and everyone was a little anxious to get the party underway. The usual *"let's get the fun started"* atmosphere was counterbalanced with a *"let's get it over with"* aura in the air.

The two Drake boys and the Gorshin boy began setting up tables and chairs and readying things around noontime and were soon joined by the neighborhood girls who were charged with stringing party lights across the property, setting out supplies of paper and plastic tableware and making sure the music was all set to go. The men, except for Jacko who, along with all the women, spent the major portion of the day cooking, busied themselves with setting up and stocking a big portable bar with ice, booze, beer, sodas and the evening's impressive lineup of world-class wines.

For the second year in a row the Meshitskys were noticeably absent from the hubbub of party preparations. Lloyd had taken his monstrous boat out earlier that morning and was yet to return. Seth was seen lurking about under his house from time to time which, as the afternoon progressed, made people even warier than they already were. Shirley and Bunny were both indoors with an inexhaustible supply of microwave popcorn, happily immersed in day-two of a holiday weekend marathon of *Roseanne* reruns.

* * *

The food started making its way out of the houses and down to the party area earlier than usual. The serious main course dishes everyone customarily prepared normally didn't appear until after the party was in full swing. But there was never a shortage of wonderful appetizers to get things underway. From Mona came fried zucchini flowers, and grilled sea scallop spiedini. Jacko and Spike brought down duck liver crostini and salmon tartare with green olive pesto. Carrie made a warm terrine of baked sausage, peppers, polenta and mozzarella. Daphne brought parmesan-stuffed baked figs wrapped in prosciutto, and Swifty made his potato salad. In addition to Rich's smoked tuna, Irene surprised everyone with clams casino that was every bit as good as Shirley's, which by now everyone knew weren't Shirley's at all. J'net Cooper pitched in with a big pot of her garlicky chicken wings and family members, friends and others from around the immediate neighborhood arrived with all manner of delectable delights. By five o'clock there were well over a hundred people there and the long-awaited party was in full swing.

* * *

Lloyd set out in his boat alone a little before eleven in the morning that Sunday. He had a lot to think about and some important decisions to make. The roar of the boat's engines blocked out anything that might be a distraction which was just what he wanted. As he raced southward toward Cooper Point he hardly noticed the other boats in or near the channel that tried their best to give him a wide berth as he sped by, almost capsizing the smaller ones with the giant wake that his boat generated, oblivious to the curses and middle-finger gestures being sent his way.

He slowed down and pulled into the last marina on the Island to gas up and have some lunch before reaching the inlet and heading out into the ocean.

He tied up at the fuel dock, telling the attendant to fill his tanks and instructing him to bring the gas bill to him in the restaurant. He lumbered off toward the combination bait and tackle shop, convenience store and short-order food counter to get lunch. He ordered two Philly cheese steak hoagies with peppers and onions, a double order of fries, a piece of chocolate cream pie and a large Coke.

"Make that a Diet Coke. Doctor's orders," he called out to the provocatively dressed, gum-snapping waitress, his eyes glued to her perfectly plump posterior as she made her way to the kitchen. During a perfunctory, free physical exam recently, one of his few remaining doctor clients made him get on a scale and it registered at 461 pounds. His blood pressure was, in the doctor's words, *off the charts* and, without even waiting for his cholesterol scores, told him he was a walking time bomb and that he'd better do something about it before it was too late. And so he would. Starting with Diet Coke.

Lloyd fished the only one of nine credit cards in his wallet that wasn't yet maxed out and paid for his lunch and the gas with it. The waitress caught him staring at her ample bosom. He shot her a lascivious smile and added a generous tip to the bill, knowing that it might be the last time he would ever use the card. Its issuing bank, along with the other card companies and about a gazillion more creditors of all kinds, was going to be stiffed.

Lloyd got back on his boat, fired it up and headed for the inlet. Out in the ocean, he was completely alone with his thoughts. Alone was the way he liked it. Which was part of his dilemma at the moment. D-day had arrived. Within a week or so he'd be gone and he was surprised that he hadn't given much thought to certain things that were only now weighing heavily on his mind. Or more accurately, on his conscience, what little he possessed. *What to do about Shirley and Bunny? Seth was no longer an issue. He was out and that was decided a long time ago. But he never once even mentioned to his wife and daughter anything about his "plan." And, as much of a nasty prick that Seth was to them his whole life, they would never stand for his leaving him behind. Not really. Plus, Bunny had a serious boyfriend all of a sudden now and that would definitely be a problem. And a double problem with Shirley. The "dropout" had to be a complete one or it would never work. That meant no contact whatsoever with anyone anymore. Bunny would never do it willingly and forcing her to wouldn't work either. She'd meet other boys eventually but that didn't solve the immediate problem. She'd do something stupid. Call him or write to him. End up blowing the whole deal! He could pretend it was just going to be a long vacation and hope she'd be okay with it at some point down the road, but what if she wasn't? And he couldn't just leave her behind with Seth, that was for sure. Even if he left a little money to help them until they could fend for themselves. They wouldn't get anything out of the property he was leaving behind, either. It was all mortgaged way beyond its real value. Plus, Shirley would never go for it, not in a million years. True, she never questioned his authority on anything before but asking her to leave her children flat and never see them again would never fly, not even with her. Damn, why didn't he think these things through before? It seemed so simple all these years. Just drop out. Why didn't he see these problems coming at him until now, when it was almost too late to do anything about them? Could he even consider leaving them all behind? Seth he couldn't care less about. Sooner or later Bunny would get herself married and get on with her life anyway. And more and more, Shirley was becoming less and less important to him. There were times when he wondered what he even saw in her to begin with. Really, why did he even need a wife now? The plain truth was he didn't. No one, not any of them, had a clue as to where the money was. Shirley and Bunny never even knew there was any money to begin with. And he never told Seth where it was. Thank god for that! So they'd never be able to find him. Never. Maybe if he left a little money for them to get a new start. A hundred thousand. But no more! Except who would be in charge? Not Shirley. Not Bunny. Between them there wasn't half a fucking brain. They'd be broke before they knew he was gone. And certainly not Seth. He'd fuck them both over and disappear sooner than give them the time of day. Goddamn faggot! He could leave instructions with someone to advise them. No, that would risk involving someone smart enough to maybe help track him down. There was only one thing he was sure of and that was that he was leaving. And the more he thought about it the more sense it made to do it all alone. He wouldn't be the first man to just walk out on a family. Happens all the time. And for a lot worse reasons than this! Exciting actually, the thought of going it alone. With all his money he'd have his pick of women. He could get himself a real looker. Like that hot little waitress. Damned exciting, actually.* He'd already burned half the fuel in the tanks and the afternoon was almost gone. There was still a few days before he'd have to make a final decision and he was feeling better about things. He banked to portside, making a wide U-turn and headed back to the inlet as the boat's deep-vee hull deftly cut through the expanse of choppy ocean. He'd make it home by sunset and, since he still hadn't reached the limit on his credit card, maybe he'd take everyone out to dinner. Smiling, he thought *that's the least he should do.*

* * *

The sun was low, painting swirls of red and purple through wispy clouds in the west sky. The party was going strong with people milling around the tables, getting their fill of an unending array of culinary treats. Rich was the bartender of the moment, busy conducting a tasting of various Pinot Noirs with a dozen or so others. Kids of all ages were darting all over the place, having their particular brand of fun as some of the desserts began making their appearance.

The hit of this year's party was a karaoke machine stocked with music of every genre that helped a procession of revelers make semi-fools of themselves to the howling delight of all onlookers. Mona had just finished a surprisingly flawless and dramatic imitation of Janis Joplin singing "*Bobby McGee.*" Marco, Max, Swifty, Jacko and his brother Hymie were in the middle of a passionate, near-acappella rendition of "*Duke of Earl.*"

Swifty, who drew the short straw and whose assignment was to keep an eye on Harry Elias this year, was scanning the crowd as he sang but couldn't find him. Instead, he spotted his wife Molly who was sitting off to the side weeping, which meant Harry was up to his old tricks again. Aside from Molly, J'net was the only one who noticed Harry dart off toward his house carrying half a platter of baby back ribs. She was too far away to stop him but she'd be sure to give him a little scolding as soon as he got back.

J'net was also the only one to see Father Kev stroll over to the Meshitsky property where Seth was perched on a picnic table, silently spying the goings-on at the party from under his house. Propped next to him on the table was his laser device which was why J'net was watching him in the first place. Just seeing it seemed to make her heart pound almost loud enough to hear. Father Kev sat next to Seth and picked up the laser, idly passing it from hand to hand as he talked. J'net, a little embarrassed at being privy to some of their history, turned her attention away from them and when she looked back a few minutes later they were gone. She thought she glimpsed the door of the shed beyond the picnic table closing and immediately felt a pang of alarm, fearful of what Seth might do with the laser in the darkened shed. Then she noticed the loathsome device still lying on the now-abandoned table. She breathed a sigh of relief, hoping Seth would forget about it for the rest of the night and not cause trouble. She spotted Harry returning empty-handed to the party. He was taking a short cut, walking under the

Meshitsky house and she decided to intercept him before he had a chance to abscond with anything else.

* * *

Lloyd was back in the bay and passing the marina that he stopped at earlier and fought off the temptation to pull in for a quick fill-up and a snack. And another look at that tantalizing little charmer. The sun was almost down and would be gone completely in less than an hour. Better to play it safe. The channel could be dangerous in the dark and the last thing he needed was an accident to occur so late in the game. He opened all three engines full throttle and headed north toward Bay Vista, the sleek boat barely skimming the water's surface and, at times, virtually leaving it. He'd be home with plenty of time to spare.

* * *

Sunset was a kind of unofficial turning point in the block party each year. Most people, having had their fill of a veritable banquet of epicurean wonders, were finished with the serious eating phase. Not so with the serious party-long imbibing phase though, which would continue for hours more. The Island's trash collectors were never less than astounded at the number of overflowing receptacles of empty bottles, mostly from wine, that awaited them at Bay Vista after each Labor Day weekend.

After sunset was also the time that people spent making their rounds through the party area, stopping at all the tables and spending time with everyone. It would be the last chance to do that for quite some time. The party started to thin out and quiet down a little too, with most of the kids disappearing soon after sampling all the desserts. The older teenagers would steal away to one or another of the Island's clubs for a last night out and the younger ones usually went up to the Gorshin's family room for a slumber-movie party. For the grownups it was a time to relax, unwind and savor the last moments of the season with those that, over time, had become an extended summer family. The party wouldn't officially end until midnight when many of the remaining diehards threw themselves, fully clothed, off the docks for the traditional cold and instantly sobering dunk in the bay.

* * *

Lloyd was nearing the southern edge of the cove that protected Bay Vista from most of the waterway's strong currents and, only as he was passing its point, did he realize that this was the day of the big party. With all that was on his mind he had completely forgotten. The little enclave was in full view now and he could see there was a big crowd. The sun had yet to complete its vanishing act and that part of the sky was awash with streaks of muted aqua, red and pink. To the east, in the direction of the party, the sky was darkening to a deep blackish blue and festive lights illuminated the area all around the Kosciusko and Gorshin houses. He could see that there were lights on in all the houses except his own which displayed only the unmistakable, erratic light show of a TV screen flickering in an otherwise darkened room. As he got closer, music was faintly audible for short moments over the roar of his engines. *I hate these people. Every fucking one of them*, he thought as he headed straight in toward his dock. *This would be the last time he'd have to put up with them and their fucking high and mighty attitudes. Two fucking years of them and their ostracizing ways is over with now. After today they'd never see him again and they could all go fuck themselves.* He eased back on the throttles and could hear the music again. He glanced at his fuel gauges. Good, a little more than one-quarter full. He looked up at the sky. He had at least fifteen or twenty minutes before it would be completely dark. *They want music? I'll give them music. Some fucking music to remember me by. Some motor-music "CPA Express-style."*

Lloyd banked to port about a hundred and fifty feet out from the docks and settled into a wide circular path in the deep-water cove, right in front of the party. He pushed forward on the throttles to about three-quarters of full speed, increasing the engine noise and sending wave after wave of water-wake crashing into the docks and bulkhead and making his neighbors' tethered boats bob convulsively like corks in a whirlpool. Round and round he went in a perfect circle, smiling to everyone on shore with each pass as all the party activity came to a screeching halt, replaced by a thundering, monotonous, nerve-wracking din and a soaking sea-splash that came cascading over the bulkhead and onto a retreating crowd. *This is going to be fun. I piss on all of you and I piss on your precious fucking party too. Here's to the end of an era, dear fucking neighbors!*

* * *

Max was into his second consecutive encore of "*That's Amore*" when they heard it. Lloyd's boat could usually be heard as far as a mile away. Max wasn't alone in uttering a few choice expletives as he turned up the volume on the karaoke machine in a futile attempt to compete with the increasing roar of the fast approaching boat. Nor was he the only one who had heard a recent news story about a boat similar to Lloyd's exploding somewhere on Long Island Sound, and privately wishing it was Lloyd instead of the poor bastard whose bloated carcass washed ashore the following week in Connecticut. But, alas, from the all-too familiar sound of the fat bastard evidently returning once again in one piece, this wouldn't be their lucky day either.

To a person, everyone at the party turned their attention to the hated craft as it veered away from the channel and into the relatively calm waters of the spacious cove that fronted Bay Vista. It was impossible to ignore it. They watched as Lloyd headed straight for the center of the gathering as if he wasn't going to stop, or even slow down. All conversation seemed to halt at precisely the same instant, some of it in mid-sentence. Eating and drinking took an abrupt, collective time-out. Just as people were seriously thinking of running to take cover the boat turned sharply to the north and came around full circle again. Like a demented beast, Lloyd started circling non-stop and, evidenced by the grin that was clearly visible each time he passed close to the docks, was deriving immense, sadistic pleasure at disrupting the party and sending it into sudden paralysis.

Realizing after about eight laps that he didn't intend stopping any time soon, people started yelling and cursing at him.

"*WHAT ARE YOU DOING YOU FUCKING MANIAC?!?*
"*CUT THE SHIT GODDAMMIT!!*
"*YOU STUPID ASSHOLE!!*
"*MOTHERLESS SON OF A BITCH!!*
"*STOP IT THIS INSTANT YOU FILTHY SCUMBAG!!*"

Lloyd couldn't hear a word. But he enjoyed the hell out of seeing everyone getting so worked up. People were running around in a helpless frenzy.

Shirley and Bunny were peering out from behind the door of their deck.

A few people started throwing food at the boat each time it made a pass close to the docks. Someone threw an empty bottle. All to no avail.

Irene was beside herself in a furious rage. She ran out to the end of her dock and started alternately thrusting her hands, which were clenched into fists except for both middle fingers, high into the air. Up and down, up and down, one after the other, reinforcing each new upward thrust with a screaming "*FUCK YOU LLOYD!*"

Lloyd then scared the shit out of everyone by coming so close to shore they thought he would crash into the dock where Irene was standing. Max was next to Marco and said "This is getting ridiculous. I think we should call the police."

The boat returned to its course a little further out and resumed circling. Max was about to go upstairs to the phone when, watching the boat come out of its latest high-banked turn on the near side of its relentless path, they saw that Lloyd was no longer visible. As the boat continued on its repetitious course to the far side of the huge circular path the cockpit came into full view again. They saw Lloyd, who looked to be crouching low between the bench seat and the dashboard.

"What the fuck is he doing?" Max asked.

"Probably ducking out of the way of all the shit being thrown at him."

The boat made two more laps that way and everyone's attention suddenly switched to Seth who, on his Jet Ski, was now tearing after it like a bat out of hell in hot pursuit.

*   *   *

The boat had made at least twenty passes and Lloyd was giddy at the pandemonium that he was wreaking on shore. He reached up and snatched a sausage out of mid air as it was sailing by and ate it in two big bites.

"Hey, that was a good guinea-wop sausage. Must be from Mona," he yelled on the next pass. "How 'bout a beer to wash it down, dear neighbors?" he howled, laughing like a crazed hyena as he sped by again. He brought the monster boat perilously close to the docks on his next swing around and acknowledged Irene's animated *"double-flipping of the bird"* by giving her a big toothy grin and flipping one of his own right back to her.

After that brief detour, he resumed his original circular route at a safer distance and decided it was almost time to call it quits. He didn't want to chance running out of fuel. *Just a few more laps,* he thought as he felt his grip slipping on the slick chrome steering wheel. *Sausage grease,* he said to himself. From the *"grease-ball" lady's sausage,* he added, smiling at his self-entertaining wit. Lloyd wiped his hands on the shirt front that strained to cover his grotesquely protruding gut and stretched the shirt bottom out to wipe down the steering wheel as best he could. That's when he saw the red dot dancing a jitterbug all over his flabby torso. He came around again and, again, there it was on his belly, his chest, and then it was gone. *That rotten little bastard!* He scanned the party area trying to spot Seth but there were too many people and it was now too dark to tell them apart. He looked toward his house and a sudden flash of weirdly colored lightning obscured everything around it and a dull pain somewhere deep behind both eyes seized the moment. He rubbed at his eyes and tried focusing, feeling his blood boil as a white-hot rage traveled up through every inch of his massive body, through his bulging neck and into the sagging cheeks of his face. The party area was all in gray and a little blurry now and he tried again to find Seth. *I'll kill the little cocksucking son of a bitch! I'll ram that fucking laser up his fairy ass till it comes out his mouth!* Another sudden flash of lightning, white this time, bored into his left eye and made him wince. The pain was sharper than the first one and he instinctively raised his left hand to rub at his eyes again but it never made it to his face. His arm stiffened halfway there and a squeezing pain, starting just below the shoulder moved quickly down its entire length to the wrist. His arm was in an invisible, tightening vise, paralyzed. *What the fuck?* Lloyd thought, just as the explosion in his chest sent him crashing to the deck of the boat like a tripped elephant.

* * *

The scene was mesmerizing to everyone on shore. Seth, on his Jet Ski, was chasing the boat barely a few feet behind it on the unfaltering course it had settled into. He was desperately trying to get close enough to grab on to the aft corner of the boat's port side but the huge swell of the wake being produced kept him teetering back and forth as he rode its crest. Lloyd was visible to the now all-but-spellbound crowd only when the boat banked on the far side of its path and Max was the first person, evidently other than Seth, to realize what was going on.

"Somebody call *9-1-1*! It has to be a heart attack!"

It seemed like only a minute or two elapsed before Warren Blankfeld sped into Bay Vista with his siren blasting away. And only a minute or two more for another squad car and an ambulance to appear. Moments later two Coast Guard servicemen in a pontoon boat roared into the cove from the north and came to a stop just outside the boat's relentless circuit. They waved their arms and used a bullhorn to warn Seth away but their orders went unheeded. The situation was too dangerous for them to try getting any closer. They couldn't physically intervene at the speed the boat was moving.

* * *

Lloyd was twisted in the cockpit of the boat, pinned to

the deck under his weight. His right arm was wedged under and between his massive frame and the unyielding cushion of the seat, useless. His left arm was even more useless. In the fall, it had become caught in the spokes of the steering wheel and the sheer weight of Lloyd's body caused it to dislocate at the shoulder. The back of Lloyd's head was pressed against it, keeping the boat on its perfect circular course. The finger tips of Lloyd's left hand were lightly touching the top of the shaft of the port engine's throttle but, unable to reach the underside of it, he was powerless to do anything to slow the boat's speed.

Lloyd was totally immobile, totally helpless and scared totally shitless. His head was high enough to be able to peer over the seat and the port gunwale, and he could see the scene on shore for a few seconds at the top half of each arc. A Coast Guard skiff was visible during the bottom half. They were shouting something over a bullhorn but he couldn't make it out because of the engine noise. He was completely unaware of Seth keeping pace with him off the stern.

Minutes went by and nothing changed. Color was slowly returning to his vision and the pain behind his eyes had all but dissipated. The pain in his chest seemed insignificant now compared to the excruciating pain he was feeling in his shoulder. The chest pain eased, replaced by a feeling of pressure in his back and so he dismissed it as no longer being anything to worry about. He'd be running out of gas any minute and then they'd be able to come get him and tend to his shoulder. He tried putting the pain out of his mind and made himself think instead about what he'd do to Seth as soon as he got his hands on him. Then he filled his thoughts with alternating visions of that little tart of a waitress he'd just met and of his impending adventure. A brand new life. *A new life alone* he said to himself and smiled, knowing now that that would be his decision. *Yes, it would take more than a tiny little heart attack, if indeed that's what it was, to get the best of Lloyd Meshitsky, CPA, that's for sure!*

But he was wrong.

* * *

Seth knew what it was the second it happened. The very moment he saw Lloyd go down. He often thought his old man might croak from a heart attack someday. More than once recently he actually hoped for it. But not before they got to wherever it was that they were going. So what was happening now really sucked. The instant he saw it happen he raced to his Jet Ski and about a minute later he was practically touching the boat as he synchronized his speed to that of the unpiloted craft. The strong wake was preventing him from staying close enough to attempt grabbing on. He tried moving to the outside but that was worse. He needed to be able to grab and hang on to one of the boat's cleats but it was always just beyond his reach. He lost count of the number of laps they made in tandem with only inches separating them and decided this was never going to work. He needed to try something different. He had no idea how much gas his father's boat had but he knew his Jet Ski wouldn't last too much longer before running dry. He veered off and made a wide turn, slowing down to reassess his options. He saw the Coast Guard pontoon on the opposite side of the cove and knew that they couldn't do anything to stop the boat. For all he knew the boat's tanks could be full and it might be hours before it finally ran out. It was getting darker by the minute and he had to do something soon.

He watched the boat make two more laps trying to get its timing down. Halfway through the third lap he gunned his Jet Ski and headed on what looked to be a ninety degree collision course. It would have to be perfect timing to work.

A split-second too fast would see him crash at full speed into the side of the boat. A split-second too slow would make him overshoot it too far away to be able to grab on. His approach was to the boat's starboard side, the one higher in the water. It would have to be.

* * *

On shore, a fire truck and four volunteer firemen had arrived who joined the crowd watching the drama unfold as the sky continued to darken. They were all either on the docks that jutted out into the bay or pressed close to the bulkhead, the better to view the action. All except Harry, that is, who was scampering back and forth between his house and the party area with utter abandon, like he was on a free shopping spree whose only restrictions were whatever he could carry and a yet-to-be-determined time limit. Shirley and Bunny had ventured out on their deck and were standing there silently and motionless. If not for the flickering of the TV inside which cast them in eerie, back-lit silhouettes they were almost undetectable.

It was getting harder to follow what was going on as darkness continued to fall and the Coast Guard now had a powerful searchlight trained alternately on Lloyd's boat and on Seth's Jet Ski. Tension and heart-swelling anticipation grew feverishly in all who were present.

* * *

The vise which minutes earlier seemed to have a death-grip on Lloyd's now severely dislocated left arm suddenly materialized again but, this time, it took hold of his upper body, constricting it nearly to the point of depriving him of air. Shoulder pain was all but forgotten, replaced with a far more important concentration on continuing to breathe. He was drenched now, in a mixture of cold sweat and warm urine, both exiting his body in a rush of sheer terror that had overcome him. And he was hallucinating. He could swear he saw Seth's face peering at him over the stern of the boat.

* * *

It was nothing short of daredevil heroics. And it elicited a cheer and a round of applause from everyone on shore, albeit grudgingly from those that were his close neighbors. At first, in the waning light, they all thought Seth had gone completely crazy. The Jet Ski was going at breakneck speed, heading straight for the starboard side of the boat. They held their breath and braced themselves. They were sure that they were about to witness the self-inflicted demise of Seth Meshitsky and those who most loathed him were momentarily nervous. Not out of concern for Seth. No, many of them, in particular the *"gang of ten"* along with a few others was experiencing an admittedly shameful, yet insuppressible nadir of human nature. They stole quick glances at one another, each wondering if they were alone in their probable inability to mask the jubilation that was welling up inside. A jubilation that might just erupt upon the impending impact of the two speeding, fast-converging watercraft.

J'net stood a little apart from the crowd. She lifted her head to gaze skyward, remembering Joe's words from so long ago: *"Island Justice"* . . . *in time, The Good Lord always metes it out.*

So, when there *was* no impact, many an onlooker kept the mild dejection they felt a secret and joined the larger majority of people there on shore, in awe of Seth's daring feat. There was no denying that what they saw was truly remarkable. Those in the crowd that weren't all that familiar with him were buzzing with praise for Seth's *valor*, his *unselfish bravery*, his *fearless courage in the face of danger*, his *quickness of mind*, his *daring, take-charge grit*, his *intrepid athletic prowess*, his *selfless devotion*, his *demonstrable love for his stricken father*, and on and on.

Those that knew him better thought, *What the fuck is that all about?*

* * *

At the very last second before hitting the boat at full speed Seth turned abruptly to the left, sending the Jet Ski sailing over the water wake as he leapt off of it to the right. As the boat zoomed by he lunged at the aft-starboard corner, catching the tie-line cleat with his right hand and swinging his body around to grab hold and steady himself with his left hand. He adjusted his weight, moving up to grip the soft, vinyl padding that covered the aft transom with both hands as his legs floated out over the stern like two banners flapping in the wind. He dug his fingers deep into the padding, hanging on for dear life and stared at the twisted hulk of his father, wedged in the cockpit, inert but still alive and contorted in great and obvious pain.

He summoned every ounce of will he could muster to suppress a smile.

* * *

Before Lloyd realized that the face peering at him over the stern wasn't an apparition he was convinced that it was a sign sent from above. A sign meant to add to the guilty feelings that were building up at his recent decision to abandon his family. When he finally saw that it was really Seth, right there in the flesh, yelling something that he was unable to hear over the engine noise, it only compounded his guilt.

Because seeing Seth meant that his prayers were answered after all. And it was his son who had come to rescue him. The son that he'd disowned was there for him and everything was going to be alright. He was elated beyond anything he had ever felt before. The chest pain disappeared. His breathing was still a little strained but it was steady. His shoulder ached and his entire left arm and hand was asleep with pins and needles the only sensation he could feel. His hand, resting on the throttle shaft, felt as if it was three times its normal size.

Looking back at Seth, he hoped that his son was able to read the expression on his face. He hoped he was conveying the hodgepodge of emotion he felt toward him at that moment: *Thankful for his coming to his aid, especially after treating him the way he did the past two years; Pride in the selfless character his son was displaying; Shame that he could even think of writing him off the way he did; Sending a silent promise to be his best friend again as soon as he was out of this predicament.*

He couldn't hear what Seth was trying to say to him. He could see that he was struggling to keep from falling off. The engine propellers were directly below him and one wrong move would spell disaster. Seth couldn't manage to climb aboard at the speed the boat was traveling and Lloyd was unable to gain the leverage he needed to grip the throttle and slow the boat down. There was no feeling whatsoever in his hand and his fingers were as stiff and heavy as clay. *The gas should have run out by now, damn it!* He looked at Seth and tried mouthing a message to him: *Hold on son, the engines will conk out any minute.* He hoped he understood but he wasn't sure. Seth was mouthing something back to him, slowly and emphatically. Lloyd concentrated, trying to read his lips. And read them he finally did.

WHERE-IS-THE-MONEY??

In the blink of an eye it was all gone. No more warm

fuzzies. No more tender, loving feelings for the son that moments ago he thought was there to save him. No more rekindled kinship. No more anything. Poof! Gone.

Lloyd sneered at Seth with a newfound understanding of just how evil he was and with virulent hatred in his eyes. *The rotten little son of a bitch!* He knew his fingertips were touching the throttle shaft. At least they were before they, and the hand they were attached to, had lost their blood circulation and fallen asleep. He knew he couldn't slow the boat down. But he could speed it up. He tried pushing down with his fingers and felt nothing. All sensation was gone below the elbow. If the boat hadn't responded the way it did he might have thought his hand was missing all together. But it did respond, lurching forward with a furious burst of energy.

The last thing Lloyd saw on this earth was Seth disappearing. The last thing he felt was another explosion, bigger this time, in his chest. The last thing he heard was Seth's eerie, pain-driven cackling. And the reason he could hear it at all was that, just seconds after lurching forward, the engines finally did conk out. The boat heaved to a rocking halt in a swell of ripples emanating outward in all directions, dead in the water. As dead as its now lifeless pilot.

* * *

The Coast Guard, closely monitoring the situation from their pontoon, wasted no time. In less than a minute they were in the middle of the drama, hoisting an incessantly cackling Seth out of the bloody bay water and speeding him toward shore. The crowd stood aghast as the emergency medical team met the Coast Guard crew at the end of the Gorshin dock. Seth was lifted from the pontoon onto the dock where they tried as best they could to stop the hemorrhaging before transferring him to a stretcher and rushing off to the waiting ambulance. Max and Rich lent whatever assistance they could.

There was a stunned silence in the crowd as the ambulance sped off and everyone's attention turned to the Coast Guard personnel who were now on board Lloyd's boat. The calmness of the crew in the darkened distance and the absence of haste displayed as they assessed the situation told those assembled everything they needed to know. A few of the women from around the neighborhood made their way up and into the Meshitsky house to be with Shirley and Bunny. Officer Blankfeld followed along with one of the firemen.

Max, in answer to someone's query about Seth's injuries said, "His whole crotch is torn apart. His penis is gone."

Father Kev was within earshot and, upon hearing this, raised both hands to the sides of his head and began to run amok, screaming *"JESUSFUCKINGCHRIST!"* over and over and over until J'net was able to catch him and calm him down. Everyone else was already calm. Calm beyond words.

Daylight had all but waned and darkness was taking control as stars began to make their first appearance in the clear, moonlit sky. Bottles and bottles of fine wine would go ignored. What remained of so momentous a night for the still-shaken residents of Bay Vista called for nothing less than strong scotch, bourbon and vodka.

J'net

It's when bad things happen to good people that make folks question the workings of the Lord the most. Course, there's never a good enough answer in those cases. It's altogether different though when rotten people get what they deserve. Sorta like justice bein' served. Or like Joe used to say, "Island Justice." Anyway, those were the thoughts goin' through the minds of many that night, me bein' included among em. That's not to say we weren't conflicted in some respects too. Mostly about Shirley and Bunny I mean. Watchin' people cope with tragedy's never fun no matter who they are. But we all have to go through those times and when the victims and sufferers ain't necessarily people you're real fond of in the first place it's a lot easier for those of us on the outside lookin' in. So, I guess that's the way most of us were feelin'. The gatherin' didn't last too much past the time that all the emergency people finally cleared out. Folks started driftin' away little by little. It wasn't a party atmosphere anymore that's for sure. Real quiet, everybody's nerves bein' shot the way they were. Understandable too, cause it was a real calamity that left all of us a little unstrung. Hard liquor was bein' had by most of the people still millin' about. If ever there was a time when straight whiskey seemed appropriate this sure was it. I knew it was late but I also knew I could use a good stiff scotch myself and that's exactly what I had. Then I had another. Reason enough, I told myself. You could almost read peoples thoughts just by lookin' at their faces. Wonderin' what was to be here at Bay Vista after the ordeal of this night. That's "Ordeal" with a capital O. Things would never be the same. That was about all that was for certain. Me, I guess I knew that my time here was over. My thoughts were filled with Joe. And Belize. And Joe Jr. Yes, I guess the events of this night were a portent of my departure from the Reach.

Fifteen
A Conundrum and Conundrum

The heat was intense when J'net deplaned in Belize City. But it felt good, warming her slight, aged body through and through. She spotted Joe Jr. right away. He was waiting beyond the tarmac near the entrance of the huge Quonset structure that was the passenger terminal. Forty minutes later, after retrieving her luggage and driving into town they were seated at the same table they were at so long ago with Joe. The outdoor area of the café hadn't changed one iota in all those years.

Waiting for their lunch to arrive, J'net told Joe Jr. the whole story of the bizarre block party. Well, almost all of it. Joe Jr. kept shaking his head, saying "*unbelievable*" as she imparted every last detail, save one. They had a wonderful lunch, and talked some about J'net's new life. She intended to live it at the little "*hut*" down in Punta Gorda that she and Joe had spent so much happy time at and that she still owned. She would be headed there the next day and planned to stop on the way for a small respite of quiet reminiscing at the jungle lodge where she first met Joe.

J'net looked across the square at the bank that Joe Jr. still worked at. The same bank that they all saw Lloyd emerge from years ago.

"I wonder if his account is still there," she said, nodding in the direction of the bank.

"I couldn't say. Without an account number it's impossible to know. If it is I'm sure his family will be accessing it in due time."

"Not if they never knew about it," J'net said.

"What do you mean?"

"I don't believe he ever told anyone about it. Not even his family. I've had enough conversations with his wife over the years, sorta hinting around the subject and if she knew she would've let on."

"You really think so?"

"I know so. That's just the sorta thing Shirley'd never be able to keep a secret."

They ordered coffee and sat without talking for a few minutes, each of them deep in thought, probably about the same thing.

J'net broke the silence. "What happens to the money if no one ever claims it?"

"Nothing. It just stays there, collecting interest."

"Forever?"

"Until someone uses the account number to access it."

"Anybody?"

"Anybody with the right number."

"Hmm." J'net mulled that information over in silence, staring across at the bank and tapping the fingers of one hand lightly on the table.

"How many digits in those account numbers?" she asked.

"Five."

"Hmm." She thought a little more. She asked Joe Jr. for a pen and took the napkin from her lap. Smoothing it out on the table, she wrote "*2–4–2–6–2*" and handed it to Joe Jr.

"I'm gonna order another cup of coffee. Why don't you run across the street and see if that number tells you somethin'. Go on, scoot!" she urged him again.

He looked at what was written on the napkin and said, "What is this?"

"A hunch," J'net answered. "Go on, check it out."

* * *

It was pleasant there at the café. Big umbrellas rejected the sun's rays and a gentle breeze was in the air making the afternoon perfect for the tourists and locals who lingered there with J'net. Less than ten minutes had passed when she saw Joe Jr. come out of the bank. He walked across the broad plaza, a little unsteadily J'net thought, toward the café. He made his way back to the table and plopped into his chair. He was as white as a ghost. He looked around at the people seated at the other tables to make sure they weren't staring at him. He loosened his tie and unbuttoned the top of his shirt, the better to breathe.

He opened his hand which held the crumpled napkin and whispered, "What *is* this?"

"A conundrum and conundrum," J'net answered rather brightly, adding "So I guess I was right."

"A conundrum and conundrum? What does *that* mean?"

"Well, your question is a conundrum and the answer to your question is also a conundrum. So, conundrum and conundrum. Now answer *my* question. I was right, wasn't I?"

Joe Jr. was speechless. Once again he nervously glanced around. He tried to say something but couldn't get a single word out.

"How much?" J'net asked, smiling warmly at her stepson. No response. "How much, darlin'?" she asked again, reaching across the table to put her tanned, withered hand over his which still clutched the balled-up napkin.

"N-N-N-N . . ." He couldn't say it. He tried again. "N-N-N-N-N . . ."

J'net

Joe, here we are again. Back here where it all started. The monkeys are doin' their serenade again. Seems louder than ever before. I think the waiter thinks I'm a little tetched in the head. I wish you could've seen the look on his face when I asked him to set the extra scotch on the table across from me, right there at the empty seat. Maybe you can see. I don't know how that works. Seein' things from up there where you're at, I mean. Guess I'll be findin' out for myself soon enough. If "up" is the direction I'll be headed in, that is. We'll learn about that in due time I guess. Well, if you truly can see then you already know what's been goin' on. Somethin' huh? Funny how things work out sometimes. It took a few extra days for me to get to the lodge, what with all that was goin' on up in Belize City with Joe Jr. Goodness, it's understandable. I mean, havin' over nine million dollars fall in your lap like that sure can have an effect on a person. He's calmed down now. And the best part is that he decided to go back to the Reach. Full time. With his friend Joe of course. He's pickin' up and goin' with him. Says now that money's not such a problem he'll be able to shift his little design business up there. They're plannin' to live right at the house at Bay Vista too. We spoke to all your old pals the other night. They were good friends to you, Joe. Drew and Roland and Lars. They're gonna be good to Joe Jr. too, I can tell. Promised to teach him the ropes and get him started so's he don't make too many mistakes. Imagine, Joe Jr. pickin' up where you left off. Another generation of Coopers developin' projects on the Reach. Sad though, too. Maybe you saw the tears in his eyes when he said he wished he could've done it with you. I hope you did. Anyway, there's more good news. Seems that the Cooper name might not be dyin' off on the Reach any time soon after all. They're thinkin' about adoptin'. They'll be travelin' for a month or two before goin' back. Seein' a little bit of the world. Includin' some of he underprivileged parts. Maybe find a needy orphan baby in poverty somewhere that they can give a better life to in the U.S. of A. Maybe even more than one. Lord, it makes me chuckle listenin' to them two go on. Joe, if I were you I wouldn't be surprised if future generations of Coopers on the Reach are a tad darker skinned than they are at present. Or maybe slanty-eyed. Or both! No, I wouldn't be surprised at all. He really is a good person, Joe. I know you're happy for him. I sure am. Well, if you've been watchin' then you know the rest of it too. About "Island Justice" I mean. It's true that the Good Lord always metes it out. Sometimes, though, maybe he needs a little help along the way. Course, I don't know if what I did nudged him a bit or not. I sorta like to think that I did. The important thing is that the swine is gone from the Reach. That's all that really counts, right? I hope you're not mad at me, Joe. Or worse, disappointed in me. And I sure hope you're not cross with me when we meet again. I suspect that time ain't all that far off. Till then, my love.

* * *

J'net sipped the last of her scotch and looked around the rooftop terrace. The lodge wasn't crowded this time of year. She was alone with the vibrant sounds of jungle life, dominated by hundreds of howler monkeys, coming from all directions beyond the terrace perimeter. She spent a moment gazing at the glass of scotch sitting on the table across from her, its amber contents still undisturbed. She raised a forefinger to her lips and gently kissed it. Reaching across the table she touched it to the rim of the glass and let out a sigh. She rose from the table and walked to the railing of the terrace and looked back to see if anyone was there. Satisfied that she was alone, she loosened the draw strings of her large sack purse, rummaged around inside and found what she was looking for. She brought her hand out and studied the object for the first time. Black, sleek and cylindrical, slightly longer than her hand and heavy for its size. She reached back and, with all the strength that was left in her nearly eighty-year-old arm, threw it as high and as far as she could over the nearest treetops. The monotonous chatter of the jungle ceased the instant the laser started falling through the trees, noisily bouncing off of snarled limbs and continuing down for what seemed like minutes through the dense, black vine and underbrush. It finally hit the ground with a soft thud, followed by an eerie silence. Only after they were certain that the intrusion was over did the denizens resume their incessant prattle.